Edith Stewart Drewry

On Dangerous Ground

A Novel: Vol. I.

Edith Stewart Drewry

On Dangerous Ground
A Novel: Vol. I.

ISBN/EAN: 9783337066789

Printed in Europe, USA, Canada, Australia, Japan

Cover: Foto ©Andreas Hilbeck / pixelio.de

More available books at **www.hansebooks.com**

ON DANGEROUS GROUND.

A NOVEL.

BY

EDITH STEWART DREWRY,

AUTHOR OF "A DEATH RING," "SWORN FOES," "BAPTISED
WITH A CURSE," "TWO FLOWERS," ETC., ETC.

IN THREE VOLUMES.

VOL. I.

LONDON: F. V. WHITE & CO.,
31 SOUTHAMPTON STREET, STRAND, W.C.

1883.

CONTENTS.

CHAPTER X.

CHAPTER XI.

CHAPTER XII.

CHAPTER XIII.

CHAPTER XIV.

CHAPTER XV.

CHAPTER XVI.

CHAPTER XVII.

CHAPTER XVIII.

CHAPTER XIX.

CHAPTER XX.

ON DANGEROUS GROUND.

CHAPTER I.

AN ODD ADVERTISEMENT.

A HOUSE in a quiet street in the west central district, a small parlour, modestly furnished, and a woman pacing to and fro its narrow limits with a quick, restless step, to which one glance at her face, with its lines of care and suffering, gave a deeper, sadder meaning than mere impatience of mood or passing fretfulness at the perpetual patter of the rain in the dreary street

outside—all the more dreary in the growing gloaming. Singularly incongruous and
out of place, too, she looked in the dingy
parlour, this superbly handsome woman,
rich in the majestic beauty of her five-and-
twenty years, perfect grace and ease in
every turn, every movement of the tall
slight form, in the carriage of the small
finely-posed head—the stamp of that blue
blood which only ages of birth and culture
can give and no gold can buy, thank
Heaven !

One action of hers told a story, for twice
in her restless walk she paused to look at
her left hand, on which a wedding-ring
glittered ; and the second time struck it
almost passionately with her right, and
wrung them in mute anguish, then turned
sharply as with a slight tap the door
opened, and a little round, good-natured
looking body came in with some journal
in her hand.

" Good morning, ma'am ; the boy's

brought your *Athenæum,* and I hope there'll be something in it for you *this* time—not had no success, I suppose, my dear?"

Mrs May's beautiful tenant shook her head.

"No, Mrs May, it's all against me—this being married—they all draw back when it comes to that miserable fact; it is no use to tell them that I have a legal separation, and that Mr Albany cannot molest me, or refer them to my lawyers in proof of that and a reference for myself; and you know, Mrs May, that all the two years I have been your tenant — poor Professor Merton's secretary — I have never even known where my husband was, and do not now."

"It's a cruel thing, ma'am, I do say!" said the little landlady indignantly, "and you got your marriage lines and all, and so clever and handsome too, and such a one to work too, and the poor dear blind professor dead three months, and you can't get no work! It's a right down cruel shame, Mrs Albany!"

The other stood looking down on her for a moment, and then said with a heavy sigh,—

"Everything is so fearfully overcrowded now-a-days, secretaryships are especially close, and for teaching, as I say, ladies (and I don't blame them) are naturally shy of a woman, the more so if she has good looks, who is a separated wife. I tell you plainly, Mrs May, that, as things are now with me, I shall not be able to stop on here long, for I will starve before I owe—especially to a hard-working woman like yourself."

"Now, Mrs Albany, I can't a-bear such words!" exclaimed the landlady; "something must turn up soon! Why, there might be something in that there very paper! Surely every one won't mind the marriage. I wish you was a widow outright, I do!"

So perhaps in her secret heart did Gabrielle Albany, but she only took up the *Athenæum* listlessly enough, and ran her eyes down the first advertisement columns. The next moment she started, with a half uttered exclamation.

"What a strange advertisement! Listen, Mrs May. 'Wanted immediately, an accomplished woman, who will act as companion to a young lady, and also as secretary, and to be generally useful to a semi-invalid. Applicant must be a married woman. Highest references exchanged. Address,' etc."

"Why, ma'am!" cried out the little May excitedly, "that's just cut out for you; did you ever now! You answer it, and my son shall post it, quick."

"Thank you, dear Mrs May; but there is no such desperate hurry, as, being after six, my answer could not reach till tomorrow morning. The address is, 'G. L., Great Western Hotel.'"

"Well, ma'am, you ring when your letter

is ready," said Mrs May, nodding emphatically, "and it shall go ;" and off she trotted like a good-natured little barrel on legs, while Mrs Albany opened her desk, not, however, with any expectation of even a reply ; she had suffered and knocked about the world too much to expect anything. She wrote full particulars so far as business necessity required, and named her lawyers and the widow of her late employer as references, and when her letter had gone there was nothing to be done but wait ; indeed, she put the whole matter from her mind as much as possible, though now and then she wondered why the applicant must be married.   Was the "semi-invalid" of the male persuasion ?   Perhaps possibly some boy of eighteen, whose anxious mamma was afraid of his falling in love ?

"Bah ! what matters it ? " she muttered bitterly ; " I would give this right hand to undo that one fatal, miserable mistake of nine years ago."

Nine years! Had she been then only a child of sixteen when the shackles of a cruelly disastrous marriage were laid upon her? Whose had the fault been? At whose door lay the wrong? Surely, with those who had left her year after year, a poor little neglected thing, in a dreary school that was simply a cold, harsh, loveless prison house, to the wild, free, high spirit it could not break or tame, but only madden into desperate recklessness; and so, when handsome, wicked Leicester Albany crossed her path, and whispered of his love, and of freedom with him in foreign lands, she, mere child of just sixteen, saw only the escape, and fled with him, bound once and for all, wedded for life before she knew or dreamed what heavy chains she had put upon herself.

Saturday passed without any answer; all Sunday, of course; but on Monday morning came a letter, in a regular lady's hand.

" Lady Glen-Luna presents her compliments to Mrs Albany, and would like to see her at eleven o'clock precisely. Great Western Hotel."

And exactly at eleven Gabrielle Albany was at the hotel, where a waiter at once conducted her to a private room and left her.

But she had not long to wait, when the door again opened and admitted, not a tall, stately dame, but the smallest, daintiest, prettiest of little matrons, whose rounded form, piquant face, and glossy brown hair might pass for anything between thirty-five and forty, and young for that. It was not till such rare moments in which you could catch the face in absolute repose that it might strike a close observer that the smiling lips could settle thin and sinister, the eyes, without their sparkle, look that cold, cruel grey whose glint is hard as steel, pitiless as the nether millstone. Something of its glimpse Gabrielle caught as she entered, in the second before she spoke, rather effusively.

"Mrs Leicester Albany, I presume. Pray, be seated again, for really," with a ringing little laugh, "you make me feel like church and steeple; pardon my rudeness; but you do, indeed. I always think I must look absurd beside you tall people."

It was impossible to help smiling, and Gabrielle put up her handkerchief, apologising.

"Oh, don't apologise, Mrs Albany; by-the-bye, didn't you think the advertisement a very funny one?"

"Say original, madam," corrected the woman of the world with a slight bow, "and we shall better name it."

"Ha! ha! well, original, then; my husband and I drew it up, for you see we required a rather exceptional thing; a widow wouldn't do, we don't like widows, and a spinster wouldn't do a bit, because I want a lady who can chaperon my daughter Jessie when I cannot; and so that only left us to find, if possible, some married woman whose husband was perhaps in India, or who, for other considerations, you see, would part company, then your answer came most *apropos.*"

The lady paused for breath; Mrs Albany's low, rich voice, so soft and mellow, came quite as a relief after those quick, high-pitched accents.

"Who then, madam, is the invalid of whom you spoke?"

"Well, he is not really an invalid at all," answered Lady Glen-Luna, "but he might be, dear boy, and it is really more on his account we are making this addition to our household, as he requires a secretary, companion, possibly a nurse—you understand—some one who will be kind and useful generally. He is Sir Arthur's son—only son by his first wife—only I call him my boy, you see, because I'm so fond of him, such a fine young fellow; and a year and a-half ago, on returning from the Continent with a friend, there was one of those horrible railway accidents, and, in saving a man who was in the same carriage, my darling boy was seriously injured by something falling across his spine, I believe ; but all the doctors haven't got at the exact mischief yet, though they all say he will recover in time, and certainly he is better, for he could not for a twelvemonth even stand, and now he can just for a few minutes. And being a married woman yourself, Mrs Albany, you would not mind being so much alone with my poor Douglas, going out with him, and all that."

"On the contrary, Lady Glen-Luna, I should only be glad if I can in any way lighten or alleviate a misfortune doubly terrible to a young and active man."

"Thank you ; well, then, Mrs Albany, it rests with you to accept or refuse this situation, at one hundred pounds a year and all travelling expenses. I went myself on Saturday to your references, and am perfectly satisfied, and so were your lawyers."

Gabrielle half smiled.

"If so, madam, I am. How soon do you wish me to join you, or follow?"

"I shall return to Luna Park at once; here is the full direction, and if you could follow me in a week—"

"In two days if you like, madam."

"Oh no, no, that would be hard on you; say Thursday, by the train leaving Paddington at twelve, and the carriage shall meet you."

'A few more details were settled, and the two women parted, the younger certainly not very favourably impressed by the elder, and especially not impressed by a belief in her great affection for her stepson, Douglas Glen-Luna.

CHAPTER II.

THE MAN WHOSE WIFE SHE WAS.

GABRIELLE ALBANY started homewards as she had come, by train, glad that she had some good news to carry back to kind little Mrs May.

As she came up out of Portland Road Station, and struck southwards, she passed quickly across the head of a hansom just as it drew up at the station, and its occupant sprang out. She neither saw him nor turned, but the gentleman, as he paid the cabman, caught a full view of her as she crossed the road, and with a start and muttered " By Heaven! what luck!" swung round sharply and followed her at a sufficient distance to keep her in view amongst the people; the tall, slight figure, with its free easy grace of movement, was easily distinguished amongst hundreds. *He* would have known it amongst thousands, this handsome dashing-looking man, whose short thick beard and moustache almost entirely concealed his mouth, that feature on which of all others the worst passions and a dissolute life soonest and most indelibly set their stamp.

His chase was not a long one, for she walked fast without seeming to do so, and, presently turning up a quiet by street, paused at a door, and drew out a latch-key.

Now was his time; he strode forward up the steps and laid his hand heavily on her shoulder. In the moment that she heard the steps behind her she turned and met the free, bold gaze of those black eyes which is in itself an insult to a woman, and the passionate blood flushed to her brow, leaving her again deadly pale.

" Leicester Albany ! "

Only those two words under her breath ; neither cry nor start outwardly.

" Ay, you didn't expect to see me, I guess, did you ? " said the man coolly. " I've been trying to find you out for a month past. I must speak to you, my dear, in there, unless you prefer passers by for listeners."

She looked full in his face, and said, with a cool deliberate scorn that made even him wince,—

" I could have hated you were it not that I despise you utterly ; I could curse the hour you ever saw me, but that the mere thought of such a noisome reptile as you is contamination. Follow me—I will give you ten minutes."

She opened the door wide, and pointing to the parlour, drew back for him to pass on, followed, and carefully closed the door.

For a minute those two stood facing each other in silence within arm's-length, she steadily, unflinchingly, though the haughty blood mounted slowly again under the bold gaze of free admiration that came once more into Leicester Albany's eyes.

"By the Lord!" he said, "your are handsomer than ever, Gabrielle, and after two years' separation your beauty comes back quite fresh. I could almost play the *rôle* of lover again. One touch, ma belle, for auld langsyne, one kiss of those sweet warm lips, though you are my wife—so."

The movement was even quicker than the word, for, with it on his lips, he threw his arms suddenly around her slight form, drew her forcibly to his breast, and stooped to take the kiss to which he had long lost all right. But the false lips never touched hers, for she started from him, with a low cry of horror, flinging him off with a strength that made him even stagger.

"Stand there!" she said, with stern and haughty passion; "if there is by chance one remnant of manhood left in you save its

outward form. Your wife!—yes, God help
me!—so I am, because the Church Catholic,
which made me so, rightly makes the bond
indissoluble; but from the hour I was
forced to leave you, we are married only in
name. Your presence, your touch, your
kiss are more polluting, more degrading to
me than that of another man, who at least
would not have to see every vow taken at the
altar lying in a shattered mass between us.
Love, faith, cherish—those were your vows,
and how did you keep them during all the
long, heartbreaking seven years I lived with
you, until, merciful Heaven! I was no
longer safe with you, my husband? For
'love' you gave only the brief, ignoble passion of a few months, such as you gave to
any other mistress of the passing hour.
For 'faith' you wrote 'infidelity,' for
'cherish' and 'honour' you flung me, in
all my youth, amongst your *roué* companions for your own base ends, hurled me
into every temptation; sold your honour

and mine at last to the highest bidder in that wild place ; and when I threw myself on your breast, and clung to you in frantic terror for protection, only laughed at his insult as a jest, flinging me off; and that night, when you had staked and lost all else, gambled me—your wife—away for a few thousands to the man who had won your gold ! I shot him down like a dog, in self-defence, and escaped through untold suffering and danger, but none, I call Heaven to witness, so deadly as the awful danger in which I had stood at my husband's side, and from my husband's hand ! This creeping, despicable reptile, whom the very beasts of the field and the fowls of the air might put to shame."

This outraged woman's scathing, superb scorn was terrible, and the man shrank, and for a moment almost cowered, before it, as if he were lacerated by a hundred scorpions. Dastard like, he took refuge in a fierce sneer, when he could face her again.

"Then, since the chain that binds you still to Leicester Albany sits so heavily, and perhaps you have good reasons to wish for freedom, eh?—why did you not do the thing thoroughly while you were flying to law, forsooth?" In the mere sound of his own voice he was regaining his bold effrontery once more. "You best knew how very easily you could have got a divorce, — and — could — now!" How he watched her, as the words dropped slowly from his evil lips! "It is not too late. I haven't been a saint after, any more than I was before, you fled from my protection. Appeal to the law again, ma belle. I shall not stand in the way; it may go by default, as the judicial separation did. You had it all your own way then, and may again for me."

"Now, I see why you have been trying to find me this month past," said Gabrielle coolly, and fixing her dark eyes steadily on his face. "Your whole appearance plainly

tells me that at present you have plenty of
money at command. Homburg and Monaco
have been propitious. You are a gentleman
so far as birth, education, society manners
go ; in nothing else. You are still handsome, and certainly, even at five-and-thirty,
do not look the dissolute *roué* you are ; perhaps because you never drank ; that would
have soon disordered your hand—*n'est ce
pas ?* With all this, you might, you think
(correct me if I make any error in my state-
ment) easily make some good match, an
heiress perhaps, or a rich widow, if—ah,
that obstinate little word !—if it were not
for the simple obstacle of this marriage, "
touching her wedding ring. "Bigamy is
such an ugly word, isn't it ? If the wife
should chance to hear of the affair—so
vulgar too, and ridiculous for dashing
Leicester Albany ! You thought it would
be far better and safer to first rid yourself
of this obnoxious marriage and wife, who,
despite all your kindly efforts, would not

be driven to exchange your ' protection ' for
that of another man. As that so signally
failed, and as your own conduct was so
black that no charge of wrong against her
could have stood its ground, even if true,
the only next move possible was to try and
get the wife to avail herself of your miserable
cruelty and unfaithfulness."

" In the devil's name, then, do it, and
free us both ! " Albany broke in, with a
fierce passion, before which most women
would have quailed ; but her firm lips never
quivered, the delicate hand resting on the
chair-back near her never shook a hair's-
breadth, though her manner changed.

" If," she said, bending forwards, " I believed in this monstrous iniquity, which is
now a living disgrace to England, this
modern pest-house which helps to make
such men as you, and such women as you
would have made me, if it were really
possible for man to break what God
made, for any law of man to put asunder

what God joined together, and only God
can loose by death—if only one word of
mine could set you free to wed again, I
would not speak it, because I would not
put it into your power to wreck another
young life as you have mine—perhaps to
drive another, weaker mentally and physically than I am, into the sin from which
I escaped by almost a miracle. For myself,
you have taught me so terribly what a
hell on earth marriage may be, that I have
no wish to try it again, were I free ten
times. As far as you are concerned, the
law has done for me all that I want; it
has absolutely freed me from you, save in
the mere fact of bearing your name, and
being (literally only in name) your wedded
wife. You are even liable at this moment,
if I choose it, to arrest for contempt of
court for forcing yourself upon me here.
Saving that one unbreakable link of marriage, I have severed every tie, destroyed
every vestige, every letter, or writing, or

likeness that would recall your existence
to me."

A sudden gleam leaped into his black
eyes, but he only said, with a sneer,—

"Then you had better drop my name
since you so despise its owner; and we
should at least be strangers if ever or
wherever we might meet."

She looked straight into his eyes, and
said steadily, deliberately,—

"I will NOT. I am your wife; and I
warn you that whatever evil scheme you
form I will foil you. Go; the ten minutes
are more than spent."

She flung the door wide, and stepped
back; gathering her robe aside, stood motionless until the street door clanged behind
him, and then—then threw herself on the
couch with a terrible burst of agony, as God
send few indeed may know.

But Leicester Albany, even in all his
rage and disappointed fury, laughed to himself as he strode away. No one had seen

him there, and she had destroyed everything that could identify him.   It was only
her word against his !

What was the desperate scheme that
had flashed into his mind when that fatal
admission was made by his unfortunate
young wife.

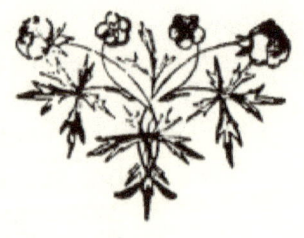

CHAPTER III.

DOUGLAS GLEN-LUNA.

IT was with a heavy heart after all, and no great hopes for the future, that Gabrielle Albany parted from good Mrs May, and started for this somewhat odd situation, and certainly to her, in many respects, quite new experience. Fortunately it was one of those lovely days which make everything, physical and mental, wear its brightest aspect; and it soon had its effect on a mind and temperament singularly strong, finely balanced, and elastic and impressionable indeed as a Southern's.

The railway journey took up full two

hours, which brought her into the quiet little station of Doring between two and three o'clock—a pretty little toy-like station, with white railings fencing it from the high road so exactly like the sheepfolds of a child's farmyard, that you almost looked for the inevitable brown - spotted cow, feeding eternally, and the brown Dobbin, and the yellow cat sitting on her tail, and nearly as big as horse and kine. Beyond that the silver river glinted and rippled, with glimpses of rich wooding and hill and dale.

Did the river flow past Luna Park? the traveller wondered, as she stepped on to the platform, and gave the provincial-speaking porter the description of her luggage. But she had no further trouble on that point; for before it was well out on the platform, a man-servant, in a handsome livery of blue and silver, came out from the station, glanced round, and came straight up to her with a respectful salute.

" I beg pardon, madam ; but are you the lady we are expecting at the hall ? "

" My destination is Luna Park, certainly," answered Gabrielle, smiling, " and my name is Albany—Mrs Leicester Albany."

" That is right, then, madam. I have the waggonette waiting, and will see your luggage safely in it, if you would kindly sit down a minute."

" Thank you."

The man touched his hat again, and went off to the porter, who, of course, knew him well enough ; and Mrs Albany, giving up her ticket, passed outside, where stood a well-appointed waggonette and pair.

A few minutes more and they drove off, the servant remarking that they should soon reach the park gates. In fact, getting to Doring high road, the man took a turning which led straight on about a quarter of a mile up to some very handsome iron gates, with a pretty lodge within. Passing through these gates, the carriage drove on through a stately park, and presently came in view of a noble old hall, with a sweep of terrace facing, as Gabrielle now saw, the river, which flowed at the bottom of the grounds, and lawns surrounding the mansion. The avenue of trees up which the carriage had come, however, led to the grand entrance round to the west side of the building, and there the servant drew up, and assisted Gabrielle to alight, as soon as the peal he gave the bell brought a footman to the door; then drove away with her luggage to another entrance, whilst she was shown across the wide and magnificent hall, along a corridor, and into what looked like a breakfast or morning room.

In a few moments there was a rustle of silk outside, a bright, clear, if somewhat metallic, voice she knew, saying to some one,—

"Yes, of course; up to her rooms, and send my maid here," and Lady Glen-Luna entered.

"I'm glad to see you again," she exclaimed, in her pretty, effusive fashion, which most people thought so charming. "I hope you have had a pleasant journey, Mrs Albany; if, indeed, such a tiresome thing as a railway journey can ever be pleasant."

"I generally manage to beguile the longest journey, Lady Glen-Luna," answered Gabrielle, amused, if not more prepossessed than at first, at her little ladyship. "I am, you see, so used to travelling in all sorts of odd ways and places, that nothing comes amiss to me."

"Why, that is just like my dear boy!" cried the little lady, delightedly; "he is just such a cosmopolitan. Oh! you and he will get on capitally, I'm sure! Your rooms are in the west wing, near his, for," laughingly, "you belong to his suite, you must understand, not to the general household. Oh! you hold a position of importance; you are principally Douglas's secretary. Jessie can only have a little bit of you when her brother chooses to spare you. Here comes my maid Powell; she will show you your rooms, dear Mrs Albany, and do anything you wish for you; so ta-ta for an hour."

Mrs Albany's bent head and curved lips thanked her with the most graceful courtesy; Mrs Albany's inward cynical comment was— "I wonder what all this means! It glitters a little too much to be all real gold!"

The thought, the distrust, the quick insensible suspicion of false coin somewhere might perhaps be a little cynical, the outcome even of a nature slightly seared by the bitterness of its worldly experience; but, for all that, the subtle impression of insincerity had taken hold, and would not be shaken off. It had no shape; it was "without form and void;" but it had struck root, like the mustard seed, which is the smallest of seeds, and would grow day by day into a great tree.

She followed Powell along corridors and

galleries, and up this staircase and down that
—all familiar enough to her later—until
they emerged into a fine wide hall on the
ground floor, opening to the grounds by a
double door, with a lift to the floor above,
and a wide, shallow stone staircase, also
leading to the gallery which ran round the
top.

" Now, madam, we are in the west wing,"
said Powell, ascending the staircase to the
first floor, and passing on to a stately corridor; " all our Mr Douglas's suite of rooms
are here, in the left, facing the south, you
see, ma'am, and the river; and your apartments are on the same corridor, near the
end, because, as my lady said, you belong to
Mr Douglas."

Which, in the eyes of the dependents of
the house, was evidently a great feather in
the cap of any so greatly honoured an
individual.

The maid, as she spoke, opened a door and
ushered the new inmate of the west wing

into a spacious and luxuriously-furnished sitting-room, from which an inner door admitted them to a large, elegantly-appointed bed-chamber, where Gabrielle found that her luggage had preceded her, and a dainty tray with refreshments and tea awaited her. Powell placed an easy-chair at the little table, and poured out a cup of tea, remarking that she was sure Mrs Albany must be quite faint, and as dinner was not till seven, she hoped she would eat. Could she unpack anything? What would she wear?

"Thank you, Powell." She did not know how her own beauty and winning voice and manner had won their way already. "All I want for to-day is in that black trunk, and this is the key; and I shall take but little time dressing, as you see my hair is all curly by nature, only on to my shoulder, so that I really need not trouble you further."

"Indeed, madam, it is no trouble, but a

pleasure, to wait on you," answered Powell, busy over the black trunk, from which she drew first and foremost an elegant dress of rich black satin, trimmed with crimson. No doubt, in the process of dressing, Gabrielle could have learned the whole history and doings of the family, from A to Z!; but she had no inclination to hear the talk or gossip of the servants' hall, and only asked a few questions about the neighbourhood, the *locale* of the river,—of course there were boats, and so on ; and, by the time she was ready for introduction to such members of the family as were indoors, the hour had elapsed, and a tap at the door, and Lady Glen-Luna's chirrupy metallic voice asked,—

"Are you ready? May I come in ? Yes ?" as Powell opened the door.

"Ah, pardon me, my dear Mrs Albany, I never *can* stand on ceremony, you'll find, but how exquisite you look in that sweet dress ! So becoming to your style. I hope you like your rooms, and the piano. Well,

as neither Jessie or Sir Arthur are in from
riding yet, shall we go to see my poor boy?
I daresay he'll like to see his new secretary."
And, sooth to say, Gabrielle Albany had a
great longing to see this unfortunate lad,
for whom her heart ached. There are perhaps few things that touch a woman so instantly and deeply as to see a young and
vigorous man stricken down in his richest
promise. There is no surer appeal to a
true woman's sympathy or heart, than to be
thrown helpless on her care.

"I want to catch him unawares before
we are seen," whispered Lady Glen-Luna
merrily, as she led the way back along the
thickly-carpeted corridor. "The anteroom
door was open just now, and by the scent
of flowers I am sure the inner one is wide
open, as well as both the windows.
Hush!"

The little lady was right, and, as they
paused beside the anteroom before the wide
open inner door, Gabrielle had before her

for a few minutes a vision, beautiful indeed to the artist's eyes, but ah, me, how painful to the woman's !

A vista of sunlight, and soft glowing colours of carpet and flowing silken draperies, and masses of flowers which flung their rich perfume over the whole luxurious apartment, colour and exquisite statuettes, and pictures, all reflected back and again in costly mirrors. All this the quick eye took in, revelling in the wealth of artistic beauty, noted too, the glimpse of a grand piano, and the light and elegant wheeled chair, that told its own sad tale, and turned with a throb of intense pain on the one living being within that room. There, right in one of the wide open bay windows, on a low couch, amongst a mass of crimson cushions, lay, not a lad's, but a man's tall slight form, motionless, as if both face and form had been those of a beautiful marble statue fresh from the sculptor's chisel ; the attitude, perfect in its easy grace, but not one of repose. The last movement had too evidently been one of restless weariness—one arm flung back above the fine head, the slender hand almost buried in the rich masses of curling burnished locks that lay ·on the silken cushions, the head itself tossed back and slightly aside, with the face quite upturned and almost deathly pale, despite the light that fell full on its delicate and chiselled beauty.

"Douglas," said Lady Glen-Luna advancing, and at the sound he started, lifted himself abruptly on one arm, and turned on the visitors a pair of dark magnificent grey eyes, heavily fringed by very long silky lashes, and how instantly the whole mobile face changed as that glance rested on the beautiful stranger.

"A thousand pardons, Adeline; I thought I was still alone."

A delicate accent, uttered by the softest, most melodious tones, a little languid, per-aps, with that subtle pathos which almost

invariably underlies a very musical voice, and
gives it, perhaps, half its power and charm.

" I saw the doors all open, dear, so I
thought I might dispense with ceremony,
and at once introduce to you your new secretary and companion, Mrs Leicester Albany."

" It is a pleasure to which I have looked
forward all this week," said Douglas Glen-
Luna, holding out his hand, and, as hers
lay for a moment in that warm, firm clasp,
oddly and suddenly the chance choice of
expression of the lady's maid flashed vividly
before Gabrielle's memory,—

" Your apartments are in the same corridor, because you belong to Mr Douglas."

" I must try not to disappoint your
expectations then, Mr Glen-Luna," she
said in her gentle way.

" Nay, I hope I shall not tax your powers
too far!" Douglas answered, with a smile
that lighted the handsome face like sunshine. " I am afraid that the *belle-mère*
has been telling some awful tales of my

severity and exacting ways." He stretched
out his arm as he spoke, and drew up a
low chair. "You are standing, and as
I see my little *belle-mère* is already pre-
paring to leave us to make friends as best
we may— Must you really go so soon,
Adeline ?" he broke off.

"My dearest boy, really ! don't you see
I am not even dressed for dinner yet ; and
so ta-ta for the present."

The young man just touched his softly
moustached lips to the white jewelled
fingers she extended, and, as she tripped
away, turned again to his new companion,
with, she fancied, something of relief.

"Well, then, Mrs Albany, since you are
to be mainly domiciled in these rooms, in
charge of such a worthless being as myself,
I must e'en do my best to make you feel
quite at home here, or"—with a quiet,
earnest look of the dark grey eyes—"may
I say to make you feel this your home ?"

Home ! a strange word to the beautiful

woman he addressed, a dream of the un-
known, an horizon, a myth, never once in
all her life a reality ; child and maiden,
wedded wife, and worse than widowed, she
had never known a home.

"Thank you," she said in a low voice, that
despite herself would quiver a little ; "I am
sure it will be my own fault if it is not so."

He shook his curly head slightly, and lay
back quite silent for a few minutes ; then
he said, without looking at her,—

"Perhaps you will find me far more
troublesome than you imagine, or at all bar-
gained for. They told you at first that it
was half for Jessie you were engaged, but now
you see it is really entirely for my *ménage*,
my behest—I, who never was patient—you
will weary of such a restless, helpless—"

Gabrielle's hand touched his, arresting
the bitter, impulsive words.

"Forgive me if I pain you, but I am
a woman, and just because you are helpless
and dependent you will never weary me ;

nothing will be a trouble or too hard that can lighten your burthen, but only my deepest pleasure. I know to the full what I am saying, and remember I am no inexperienced girl of sixteen, speaking without book, but a woman of five-and-twenty, whose whole life has been one of bitter trouble, and harsh, stern, dark experience. I say no more to you than I did to dear, blind, old Professor Merton, whom I lately served, and he was more helplessly dependent on others than, in God's mercy, I hope you will ever be. I have suffered so much, that suffering appeals to me beyond all else, in whatever form it comes before me."

Noble words of a noble heart, and Douglas covered his eyes for a moment, too deeply touched to utter more than a low, unsteady " Thank you," too sharply struck by the utter contrast between this stranger and his own flesh and blood to speak. *They* had left him always to suffer alone ; this true

woman clung to him for that very suffering's
sake and something of what held him silent
Gabrielle Albany read even then. But in
a few minutes Douglas dropped his hand,
and turned round once more with that
sweet, bright smile of his.

"And now we understand each other,
Mrs Albany; and to-morrow, may I hope
from this hour, will date for both of us a
brighter life? I know it will for me. Do
you wonder why I chose this floor for my
suite of rooms instead of those below?"

"Because," she answered at once, pointing out of the window, "here you get the
full effect of that beautiful view mapped
out; below you would feel more shut in."

"Ay, you take it exactly; and, besides,
I hate the rooms below these. They were
the schoolrooms and playgrounds, and all
that; they are not used now unless, perhaps, they have some young fry at Christ-
mas. Nobody inhabits this wing now but
me and mine; all the sleeping apartments

in use are quite away from us. Myself and
Harford—my man—and now yourself, are
the only people who sleep in this west wing
—unless there are many guests, and then a
few of the guest - chambers are ' requisi-
tioned ; ' so my father had that lift made
in the hall, which easily takes my wheel-
chair down, and all my apartments thrown
en suite. Look—behind that curtain is the
door (all wide for my chair or sofa) which
opens to my dressing-room, then my sleeping
apartment, and beyond that Harford's room."

" Does his room open from yours, then ? "
asked Gabrielle.

" No ; there, opposite, those two immense
mirrors are really sliding doors that go
back into the wall, and open into another
large *salon*, half study, half dining-room ;
but this is my favourite room, as I suppose
you will tell me you knew, without my
telling you."

" I need not be very clever to know
that," said Gabrielle, smiling, " or to see

that you are a connoisseur in art, and a musician too."

He laughed at that—such a rich, soft laugh, and answered,—

" I can retort on all points, I think, and I will prove it at the first opportunity. I suppose I shall not see you again, though, this evening, after you go down to dinner ? " This rather wistfully.

" I will come back to you, Mr Glen-Luna, directly dinner is over, if you wish it."

" No, no ; that would be selfish of me ; stop with them this evening. I cannot, must not, make you as much a prisoner as I am myself. Here comes Powell to fetch you to the drawing-room," as the lady's maid appeared ; " isn't it so, Powell ? "

" Yes, sir, please, with my lady's compliments, as Sir Arthur and Miss Jessie are with her there now."

" Ah, ça, then *au revoir*, Mrs Albany."

" For a couple of hours," she said, touching his hand, and followed Powell.

CHAPTER IV.

VERY TENDER HEARTED.

LADY GLEN-LUNA met Gabrielle at the door of the drawing-room, and in her pretty unceremonious way introduced her to her husband and daughter; the latter a second edition of herself on a rather large scale; the former a fine, powerfully-built, hearty speaking man of sixty, who was happiest hunting, fishing, shooting, and such like, and could in nowise understand how his son had always loved and lived the life of great capitals, and travelling here and there and everywhere, instead of a country life, which he knew Douglas hated like poison—the fact was, society had petted and spoiled him. Petted its handsome, brilliant favourite certainly had been, but the "spoiling" had been beyond society's power.

"I'm delighted to welcome you amongst us, Mrs Albany," said Sir Arthur, giving her hand such a very friendly shake, that it nearly wrung it off. "I hope you had an agreeable journey ;—but my little wife tells me you are an old traveller."

"I am indeed, Sir Arthur ; often, too, in regions and in a fashion that, I suppose, few women have experienced. Forty-eight hours in the saddle in the wilds of Mexico, with scarcely any rest, was not quite as comfortable as a first-class carriage."

"How dreadful !" exclaimed Jessie Glen-Luna ; "but what a rider you must be, then ! And were you alone ?"

"No," said Gabrielle, and there was a momentary pained contraction of the brow ; "I was with my husband. Sir Arthur, you have a lovely place here."

"I am glad you admire it, Mrs Albany; and, since you are such a rider, we must give you a mount, and show you far and near."

"And I assure you," laughed Lady Glen-Luna, "that you have risen twenty-fold in Sir Arthur's estimation by the discovery of your equestrian powers."

"You shouldn't tell tales out of school, love. My wife and Jessie, Mrs Albany, are very pretty riders indeed, but not as bold as I like; eh, puss?" patting his daughter's cheek. "Can't get them to follow hounds. You, I suppose—"

"Not me either, Sir Arthur. I like a wild ride, but I do not care about hunting or any country sports."

"Ah, now, what a shame!" exclaimed the baronet, holding up his hands. "You are as bad as Douglas. You are, then, urban; I am rural."

"You are lost now, my dear Mrs Albany," came Lady Glen-Luna's laughing tones again. "I suppose you have never been in this part of the country before ? "

"Never, Lady Glen-Luna; I have, in fact, been very little in England. I was born and lived in Florence till I was six years old—then sent by my guardian to a school in the west-end of London—and from there," she spoke in a very quiet, resolute matter-of-course way, "when I was just sixteen I married. I was abroad, out of England entirely for the next seven years, and afterwards, when I was Professor Merton's secretary, we were constantly travelling on the Continent."

"Ah, all that accounts for your accent being just a little bit foreign," said Sir Arthur, smiling. "You and Douglas will certainly find plenty in common, for I never could keep him in England much from the time he left college to the day he was brought home to our London house injured from that terrible accident, which was nearly two years ago ; he was eight-and-twenty."

" There is some hope of ultimate recovery, is there not ? " Gabrielle asked.

" We hope so ; the physicians all say so, and he is much better and stronger on the whole in the last twelve months, though he is sometimes very exhausted, I fancy ; but there is still something about the case which the Faculty haven't quite reached yet. I know this "—said Sir Arthur emphatically— " that I would give one thousand pounds down to any doctor who would make my noble boy what he was again."

" It is too good to hope for," said Adeline Glen-Luna, with a gentle sigh ; and, glancing tenderly at her, Sir Arthur whispered to Gabrielle,—

" She is such a soft-hearted little thing, and so fond of Douglas ; she was quite ill with terror and grief when he was brought home. It was she who suggested his having such a lady as yourself for a secretary and companion."

" Oh, was it ? " thought the secretary,

with a keen covert glance at the very
" tender-hearted little thing." " What
could be her motive ?"

But she only bowed, and was spared a
conventional lie by the announcement of
dinner, which to-day was quite *en famille.*
Conversation, however, flowed on. Gabrielle
was brilliant, graceful, wonderfully versatile,
always the clever, cultured woman of the
world and travel ; to each and all she at-
tuned herself with the winning grace of a
fine nature whose very charm was its utter
absence of the least art, or effort to win.
But after dinner was quite over she only
remained in the drawing-room a little while,
and then, saying that she had promised Mr
Glen-Luna to return, bade them adieu for that
evening, and went back to the west wing.

Five minutes after the door had closed,
Lady Glen - Luna, lifting her eyes for a
moment from her fancy work, said,—

" Well, dearest, and how do you like
Madame la Secrétaire ?"

"The most beautiful, most charming woman I have ever met," said Jessie— then she came nearer and sat down on the sofa by her mother—"but, mamma, I profess I do not understand you."

"No? why not, love?" The little white fingers worked on complacently; the red lips, ever smiling, smiled still. "Why don't you understand me?"

"Why, you did not like papa's taking it into his head to want Douglas to marry Hyacinth Lee, and you very cleverly tried to get off asking her to stay here this coming autumn."

"Certainly; because I am sure that Miss Lee has refused two good offers in these last two years solely on our dear boy's account, and if he only asked her she would say 'yes' to-morrow."

"Do you think he would, then, mamma?" Adeline laughed softly.

"He might, if she comes here and is thrown in his way. I should hardly think,

Jessie, that *you* need to be told why I do not want Douglas to marry Hyacinth or any one else."

"That is just it, mamma," said her daughter impatiently, "and yet you, your own self, have placed about him—flung at him—such a woman as this, whom you must see, mamma, it is impossible for any man to resist."

Again that quiet, intense little laugh, and fleeting upward glance.

"No one knows that better than 'mamma,' most sage little would-be wiseacre; but you quite forget, sweetest, that Mrs Leicester Albany *is married*—not a widow, but a wife."

"But that won't prevent any man falling in love with her," answered Miss Nineteenth Century promptly.

"Oh no! Oh dear, no, my love; but then I really cannot undertake to guard the heart or morals of a man of thirty. And scamps like I am sure this Albany is, always live for ever, just because every one wishes them dead. Of course," Lady Glen-Luna turned to get the fading light full on her work, " it would be dreadfully wicked to fall in love with another man's wife. Oh ! very dreadful, and sad ; and he never could marry her, especially sad," she said slowly, " as if—if he did, he would never marry at all. Dear Douglas has his faults, but one of his grandest, noblest, good points is a heart as faithful as a woman's, more than most women's ! Bah ! but why meet troubles half-way with absurd romantic fancies and anticipations of what I really have no fear of ? Ring for Dawson to light the chandeliers."

But Jessie understood mamma a little better now, and set her down as a clever woman.

So she was, for she knew how to reckon on the good as well as wrongful passions of the complex human heart. Tender-hearted little thing !

CHAPTER V.

ON DANGEROUS GROUND.

ABRIELLE ALBANY easily found her way back through the labyrinth of passages by which she had come, and regained the precincts in which Douglas had said she was to make her home.

As she reached the corridor, a tall, very powerfully-built man of forty, dressed in black, with a good-looking and most pleasing face, came out of the *salon*, caught sight of Gabrielle, and came up to her, with a profoundly respectful salute.

"I beg your pardon, madam, for the liberty of addressing you first, but there i something which perhaps you might like to know of, as only us three are in this wing at night. I am Harford, Mr Douglas's own courier. See here, Mrs Albany, this thick, red bell-pull, high up against the wall."

"I see it ; I can reach it, being tall," she answered. "What is it ? what does it ring, Harford ?"

"An alarm bell, madam," said the man, a little significantly she fancied. "It hangs high up on the clock tower, and if rung would pretty soon wake all the rest of the household away in the east wing, and the folks down in Doring too, as sure as my name is William Harford. It's as well to know all this, ma'am, that's all, when we've got some one so helpless and so very precious as the young master to take care of."

"It is, indeed, Harford ; thank you for telling me ; but what do you fear ?"—this, to try and get at the man's thought, if any definite one there was.

"Well, ma'am, there might be thieves or fifty things in a country house, you see, and one can't be too much on one's guard in this world, ma'am, where there's so many wolves in sheep's clothing."

As he said that slowly he looked up straight in her face, and their eyes met full for one moment; his searching, anxious, gauging her; hers steadfast, deep, perfectly reading the man's doubt and fear and meaning.

So for a minute she stood, and then, with a quiet, significant smile creeping over her firm, chiselled lips she asked a question.

"Have you been long in Mr Douglas's service, Harford?"

"Ever since he came of age, madam, and went travelling."

"Ah! then I suppose you are very much attached to him?"

"Well, ma'am, I couldn't say much in words," said the man simply; "but there ain't a living being I love as I do my master. I can't think how anyone that's much with him could help it. If I may make so bold, ma'am, as to say so, I'm very glad you have come, for he won't be left alone now; and he's so patient, and never complains neither."

"Sir Arthur seems fond of his son," said Gabrielle, without directly answering the last remark.

"So he is, madam; and he most generally sees Mr Douglas for a short time every day, but I think—" The man paused hesitatingly.

She laid her hand—that soft, delicate, and singularly nervous hand of hers—on his arm for a moment, and looking full into his face, said,—

"You may trust me, Harford, as you do yourself. I was a total stranger to the very existence of every one in this house until I answered that advertisement. I am a woman who has lived in the world entirely, and never had eyes or ears or one sense closed, who can see when many would be blind, and read between the lines; I understand you, and I think now you understand me. *I am absolutely in your master's service.*"

She dropped her hand and moved on with her light, noiseless step to the *salon*, which was now brilliantly lighted up. The door still stood ajar, and the moment she entered Douglas half lifted himself eagerly.

" I heard your voice in the corridor; how good of you to come back to me; and I am sure that you must be very tired; sit down in that little, low easy-chair."

" Thank you, Mr Glen-Luna "—she drew the chair into the window near him and sat down, " but I am not tired—not very, at any rate. I was speaking to your courier, Harford, outside."

" I know you were. I am sure you will like him, Mrs Albany; he is the best, the most faithful, the most unwearied of beings."

"I am sure of that," Gabrielle answered quietly; "we have quite made friends already. And what a fine, powerful man he is."

"Is he not? I assure you he lifts me up almost as easily as if I were—a child I had almost said; it is half knack, of course, and I am very light—always was for a man."

"I should think so, for though tall you are so slight," said his beautiful companion, smiling. "Harford seems devoted to you."

"Foi! you must not believe the quarter he says of me, Mrs Albany," said Douglas, colouring and laughing a little. "I don't believe he sees a fault in my very faulty self; he does his best to make me the most vain, selfish, and spoiled of mortals."

"I don't believe anything would make you that," thought Gabrielle, glancing at the handsome, loyal face, thrown out into such clear relief against the crimson cushions on which it lay, but aloud she said,—

"I like him all the better for the grand old feudal feeling, so rare and so refreshing in these days, but I suppose he comes of good yeoman stock; you, by your name, should be of Highland descent."

"C'est vrai, madame, we are a very ancient Highland race, faithful always to the Stewarts. My ancestor was a younger son and followed James I. to England, and his son, in the first year of King Charles the Martyr, married the heiress of these lands. Jessie is called after her."

"Is she? I suppose your sister is a great deal with you?"

The magnificent grey eyes drooped.

"Oh no, not much; of course they have much visiting to do, and it is so dull for her up here."

He said it quietly, but the restless movement of pain or weariness was involuntary, so restless that the cushions slipped uneasily.

Before he could even run the chance of hurting himself, by an attempt to replace them, Gabrielle was bending over him with a gentle, " Let me do it," and, passing her arm around his shoulders, lifted him so as to rest against her, while she shook and replaced the cushions. He tried to move, fearful of tiring her, but suddenly the beautiful head sank back heavily on her breast, the dark eyes closed, a moan of pain quivering over the lips, yet one loved name first on them in this half unconciousness.

" Mother ! "

Oh, how it wrung her very heart to hear that name ; to see this young, strong man, lying on her bosom as helpless as the infant whose few weeks' fitful life had died out these years ago ! And hot tears fell on the statuesque face even as she bathed the deathly brow and lips with the eau de Cologne she always carried about her. Consciousness had never quite been lost, and as her soft breath fanned the fragrant essence on his cheek, the colour came faintly back, the grey eyes opened, the lips moved.

"It is like—my mother! I thought—
is it?"

"Hush! only Gabrielle Albany."

"Gabrielle—is that? Ah, it is passing!
Lay me back; give me your hand."

She laid him gently back, and kneeling
down beside him, put her soft, firm hand
into his, which closed round it instantly;
and for some minutes he lay like that, perfectly still and silent. Then without loos-
ing her hand, the large eyes opened again
full on hers, as he spoke strongly, distinctly
now, with an emotion he could not crush.

"How good you are! Forgive me; it
was all my fault. I forgot again, as I too
often do, that I am not what I was. My
movement was too reckless, too quick, for
the spine, I suppose, and brought back
temporarily the agony of pain I used to
have at first. It is *that* no doctor has yet
quite got at. If they could—did I speak
just now? Something that pained, wounded
you, I fear; for surely— Ah, forgive me

for the tears! I would sooner suffer any pain than cause pain to any woman!"

"Oh, hush! it was nothing, only my own weakness," she said, bowing her face on the hand that still held hers. "You only said one word that—that once, for a few weeks, was mine—mother! And the bitterest sting was that I had to thank God for taking it."

Douglas made no answer in words; but, if ever the clasp of loyal hand spake more than any lexicon or grammar, his did then, and forged a chain of sympathy which no after blow could ever have severed; only presently he said softly,—

"I thought it was my mother, for a few moments. Your touch, your voice are like, oh! so like, and — and — she died when I was a boy, quite a boy! I am glad you are like her. I can talk to *you* of her, and take you to her grave."

A quick, grateful look into his face, a low-spoken "Thank you!" and Gabrielle rose.

"You know now," Glen-Luna added, as she resumed her seat at his side, "why I have never called Adeline mother?"

"I think I knew it before this," she answered softly; and Douglas understood her.

Were both not walking unconsciously on dangerous ground?

CHAPTER VI.

A FURTHER INSIGHT.

THE new inmate of Luna Park was up early, according to her usual custom, and in her own elegant sitting-room, arranging her desk and music books. Of the wondrous mass of "unconsidered trifles" and useless nicknacks and fancy articles which ordinarily spring into the light and bestrew a room in the first five minutes after a lady's pet box is opened Gabrielle had none; she cared nothing for such nonsense, and in her wandering, unhappy life had gathered about her none of those things that are simply in the way, to one especially who has no headquarters. She had never had hearth or Lares.

The family breakfast hour was nine ; that of Douglas Glen-Luna, she naturally supposed, would be later, or, at least, variable ; but just before eight there came a gentle tap at the door.

"Come in," she said, and Harford appeared on the threshold.

"Good morning, madam. The master heard you moving long ago, and sent me with his compliments to ask if you would do him the honour to breakfast with him at eight. He is always early."

"I shall have great pleasure in joining him, Harford, if you will tell him so, with my compliments. How is he ?"

"Why, Mrs Albany, more like his own bright, laughing self before the accident than I've ever seen him since it, till now. I wish you had been with us all along, ma'am ; for I believe it's half fret and loneliness—the mental suffering, you know, ma'am, that has kept him back; and of course, when a man is down like that, it's just a woman he wants about him constantly. I admit that it isn't one in a thousand that would suit Mr Douglas; and I'm equally sure, if I may make so bold, ma'am, that you are just that one in the thousand."

She smiled openly; the faithful man was certainly " a character "—an odd mixture of naïveté and shrewdness, with quick strong likes and dislikes.

" Time alone will show that, Harford. I will certainly do my best, and not lightly leave. Now, I will go to him."

Harford drew deferentially back, and Mrs Albany passed out into the *salon.* It was empty; but the inner doors were slid back, and within lay another beautiful apartment to which Gabrielle turned at once.

Not on a couch yet, at any rate, but reclining on that dainty light-wheeled chair, was handsome Douglas Glen-Luna, and his start and flush of pleasure was in itself an eloquent welcome, as she came forward and frankly clasped his hand.

"How are you this morning, Mr Glen-Luna? You had no return of that terrible pain, I hope?"

"Oh, no, no; thank you; it was all my fault. How good of you to commence your troublesome charge so early. Mrs Albany, you are surely gifted with a physical strength much above most women, especially such a slight, delicately-made woman as you are."

"I am so; but what makes you say so, Mr Glen-Luna?"

"Why, last evening you raised me on one arm, and held me so easily, so strongly without any effort or heave up. A weaker, less firm touch or hold would have much increased the agony."

"It is yet one more reason," she said, "for me to be thankful that I am so strong. It has stood me in good stead many a time in my life."

Douglas leaned his head back against the cushions behind him and said, playing with his silky moustache as he watched her graceful movements,—

"I should think you are the very coolest, bravest of mortals in danger."

"Merci bien, monsieur, for your good opinion," she half smiled, as she put his coffee cup beside him; but there was both pain and bitterness in that smile, for the dire tests to which both coolness and courage had been put so severely.

Douglas noticed both, and, with graceful ease and courtesy, turned the subject.

"Well," he said lightly, "I hope you will not need either here much, except if you dare to ride my fiery Arab, or drive a pair of blood horses in my phaeton, for I am sure you are great in both those lines, and fond of it too," he added laughingly, "for your eyes sparkle at the mere mention."

"You are very quick, Mr Glen-Luna; it would indeed be a pleasure, only, surely

you are jesting! You must not take my
powers on trust; your own favourite horses,
too."

"I do not think I need be afraid, Mrs
Albany, either for you or the horses," he
answered, pulling the stalk off a magnificent strawberry; "and I assure you I
thereby pay you as high a compliment as
I shall presently by begging you to try my
piano. Of course I have neither ridden
nor driven for eighteen months, and, save
my groom to exercise him, no one but
myself has ever mounted Hassan, my beautiful Arab. He would carry you splendidly!
And the chesnuts! Would not you like
them out this morning for a drive?"

"Mr Glen-Luna, I must answer you after
the style of Queen Anne's lady, when she
was asked the hour—'Whatever time your
majesty pleases!'"

"But your tell-tale eyes betray you,
Mrs Albany," said Douglas wickedly; and
Gabrielle laughed.

"Yours are far too keen; I must veil mine, I see, when I answer you. I suppose you drive out every day?"

"No," he said, shaking his curly head. "I have not done so; it was miserable, lonely, dull work—and—and I shrank horribly from meeting any one I had known; I have tried to shut away the outward world."

How perfectly she understood the man's feeling, how her woman's heart ached for him, and swelled with passionate resentment against the sister, at least, who should have made his life so different. How could they! oh, how could they so cruelly neglect one so gentle, so suffering, so helpless? The indignant cry had almost risen to her lips, but she crushed it, and laid her hand on his, with a touch that came like a tender, exquisitely sympathetic touch on a delicate musical instrument.

"You have let yourself grow morbid," she said very gently, "but I must change all that now."

" *Now*," Douglas repeated, " it *is* all changed already ; driving out, going in the park with you will be a pleasure, a relief. These very rooms look different to-day! They have been a prison. I had grown so weary, oh, so weary of everything ; I could not read for ever, reader as I am ; the mind wants, craves for companionship, a kindred mind, even in the blessed world of books. I could not even write half as much as my thoughts flowed, for they will not let me sit up for long at a time, and then I grew sick of my own presence. Jessie and her mother, no doubt, have so many claims, far more than mine, upon their time ; and little Jessie, too, is young and gay, and naturally likes society ; my dull rooms could only be a prison to her, and besides, my pursuits and favourites of art and literature are not hers. I should only bewilder and weary her, and she— well, it is my fault, I know—she would fret and jar every chord ; it is wrong in

me to be absurdly sensitive and morbid,
but—but—Ah, forgive me, dear Mrs Albany,
for making such a father confessor of you ;
it seems as if I had known you for years
instead of hours."

" Thank you."

She turned aside a moment in silence,
masking a deep emotion which is far more
easily stirred in those that have suffered
much than in those whose lives have been
comparatively free from trial. Those who
have wept for their own dead can more
readily weep for another's dead.

His noble self-abnegation, the very gener-
osity and utter unselfishness of his attempt
to shield his sister and stepmother, only
unconsciously laid yet more bare to Gabrielle their selfishness and neglect, over
which they threw the veil of words, as
flimsy to her as to their object, however
he might try to gloss it over to himself
and others.

" Say to me what you will," she said after

that pause. "I shall not misunderstand you, or—"

She bit her lip as the word "them" rose, and added "others."

When the servant came to remove the breakfast equipage, his master gave the order for his park phaeton and chesnut pair to be ready at ten.

"The blood horses, sir, what you have out in the carriage?" asked the man.

"Yes, Mrs Albany will drive them; and tell Harford to be in attendance on horseback, for" — he added, turning to Gabrielle with a smile—"though I would not care, I suppose you would not like the responsibility of both horses and master, at least until you are used to them."

"Thank you for your consideration, Mr Glen-Luna; certainly a pair of spirited horses are not like quiet park ponies, and the charge is far too precious to be risked to the least chance of an accident. Now, shall

I wheel you into your favourite window in the next room ? "

" You shall do nothing so—"

" Very easily accomplished," said his autocratic attendant, putting her hand on the handle of the light, silent, wheeled chair, and pushing it, with hardly more than a touch, into the *salon*, bringing it to anchor near his sofa.

" Fairly run away with," said he, laughingly, looking up in her face, " but needs must when beauty drives. I am afraid, Mrs Leicester Albany, that you have a will of your own, and really intend to make me feel its power."

" Quite right, Mr Douglas Glen-Luna, for I see there is much reformation needed in you, and there is nothing like—"

" Training up a child in the way it should go," said he, laying his head contentedly back. " Faith, fair autocrat, I have no objection to your rule—to fetters of gold and flowers."

"But the gold of the fetters is alloyed with harder, baser metal, and the flowers have thorns sometimes."

"You can't frighten me, Mrs Albany; I don't think there is much of the 'baser metal' or thorns either about you."

As he spoke, a step came along the gallery, a tap at the door, and Jessie, looking wonderfully pretty in her light muslin, came in.

"Good morning, Douglas; and how are you, Mrs Albany? Breakfast is on table."

"Thank you, Miss Glen-Luna; but, as I am an early riser, your brother kindly asked me to join him. We are going to drive out almost directly."

"Are you? I am so glad," said Jessie, so exactly with her mother's manner, that Gabrielle could well have boxed her ears. "We never could get him out much, though the doctors all said he ought to. Naughty Douglas! By-the-bye, dear, it's quite true that Mr Parker has given up his practice in Doring for the present, on account of his health, and another gentleman has come to his house and place."

"Indeed! you chattering puss; some fascinating young fellow, I suppose, for you girls to flirt with, eh?" laughed Douglas.

"Isn't he impudent, Mrs Albany? Well, to be sure, they say he *is* handsome, very clever, and—"

"Very old," put in Glen-Luna.

"No, sir; only about thirty-five."

"Dear creature; and what is the name belonging to this interesting biped — Brown?"

"You are a goose, Douglas! Brown, indeed! It's Dr Chandos Neville. We shall see him, of course, on Sunday, at church."

"Perhaps he's an infidel, my dear; sure to have funny notions if he's at all scientific or philosophic," declared Douglas, off hand, "or at five-and-thirty, of course, he's married—horrible idea!"

"Oh no ; he's not," said Jessie promptly, and Douglas fairly burst out laughing.

"Ma foi, you took care to ask *that*, then, ma'amselle."

"Oh ! Mrs Albany may flirt with him," laughed Jessie ; "she has had more ex-perience than I have, I daresay, being married."

"Your feminine tongue runs too fast, little Jessie," said Glen-Luna, as his quick glance saw Leicester Albany's wife shiver. "Run away to your breakfast, child, or father will be vexed."

"Ta-ta, then," cried Jessie, and vanished, just as Harford came in to announce the phaeton.

CHAPTER VII.

A DRIVE.

DOUGLAS GLEN-LUNA'S exqui-sitely-appointed equipage — the elegant phaeton, the magnificent chesnut horses, in their glittering silver harness—might well have been the admira-tion and envy of the country.

The wheeled chair was standing empty in the hall, and its owner already in the phaeton, when Gabrielle, in her graceful plumed hat, and drawing on her riding gloves, came out.

"Oh, they are beauties, indeed!" she exclaimed, patting the arching neck of the one nearest her, and the noble animal tossed

his head, trammelled by no cruel bearing
rein, and turning his great lustrous eyes on
her, perfectly aware not only of the caress,
but of the admiration.

Ah, how can any one ill-treat those noble,
faithful friends of man—horses and dogs!
The groom at the head looked as proud
as a peacock, and Douglas's smile was full
of pleasure.

" I think you will hardly know what to
say to Hassan, Mrs Albany, or my collie
dog, whom I hope to have back from the
veterinary surgeon ; he cut his foot the
other day, poor dog ! Of course you are
fond of dogs ? "

" Very, very fond of them," she answered,
as she stepped in and gathered up the
ribbons ; and then Harford mounted, the
groom stepped back, and the whole equipage swept off in splendid style down the
stately avenue up which she had come the
day before, Harford riding a little distance
ahead.

"I want to see Doring," said the fair driver; "it is a very picturesque little town, is it not?"

"Very; but—you are not going to drive right through Doring?" He winced visibly at the thought.

"If you will not forbid me, Mr Douglas. I want to break the cordon of morbidness that has been drawn round you; and, believe me, the ordeal will not be so terrible as it looks. Will you trust me?"

What man—least of all, the chivalrous Glen-Luna—could have resisted those beautiful eyes, that soft, pleading voice?

"How could I possibly say *you* nay?" he said. "I am always a ready slave to beauty's wishes. Forgive me, dear Mrs Albany, if I say all sorts of pretty things to you, for it's second nature; and if you only knew how dreadful it is not to have any one to say them to for eighteen months!"

It was said with such whimsical energy

that Gabrielle rippled into an irresistibly amused laugh.

"If that is such a grievance, pray make all the pretty speeches that come to your ready tongue, and I'll try to devoutly believe them real—shall I? I wonder how many compliments you have uttered in your life?"

"Oh, ma foi!—thousands, of course," said he coolly, opening his great dark eyes wide at her; "a fellow must, you know."

"Vraiment, monsieur!—so many, I suppose,

'That neither history nor song
Can count them all.'

Ah, the river! How beautiful, how tempting it looks in this glorious sunshine!"

"Would you like to drive back round to the boathouse, and have out the steam launch?" said Douglas at once.

"Oh no, thank you; not now. Is that the outskirt of Doring just ahead?"

She pointed her right hand to some dainty picturesque houses, evidently belonging to well-to-do people, bedded amongst trees and gardens giving on to the road.

"Yes; and do you see that pretty white house, covered with clinging roses, and a tiny verandah?"

"Yes." In fact, the horses' heads were almost alongside the gates. "Whose is it?"

"It was old Mr Parker's, the principal doctor in Doring," Glen-Luna answered; "but, if Jessie is right, this new man, Dr Chandos Neville, has just domiciled himself there. Look—there is a lady in the garden."

As the phaeton passed, the lady turned and saw it, and its very striking occupants.

"What a sweet-looking woman," said Gabrielle. "I wonder who she is? She looks about fifty, but she cannot be the doctor's mother; she looks so plainly a maiden lady. I should like—"

"Go on; tell me what?" said Douglas, glancing at the picturesque beauty of the woman at his side.

" Forgive me ; I was forgetting."

" What ? That you are to say to me whatever you please ? "

" Ah, no ! not that ; you are too kind. I was only going to say that 1 should like to know that lady, whoever she is."

" Perhaps she returned the compliment," said Glen-Luna.

She flushed for a moment, and then said, with a cynical bitterness, the more intense from its quietness, " She will not if, or when, she knows what I am. Women are merciless on a wife separated from her husband ; it is always her fault."

" I am afraid you are right in the main ; but," he said, with a flash in the grey eyes, " no one had better say so to me."

" Why not ? " she said quickly, with the same ring of intensely bitter pain in her low, mellow tones. " After all, what do you know of me or my past life, but what has come from myself ? "

" Nothing, certainly," was the quiet answer; " neither do I wish or care to know anything from any other source. And of yourself I judge for myself. I have never yet been deceived, and I am not now."

The deep grey eyes were looking dreamily out before him as he said that, as if they saw afar off, into that past life to which she had alluded—into the untold misery and cruel wrongs that had so terribly embittered, perhaps well-nigh wrecked, her young life. She made no answer for some minutes; but the firm hand on the reins shook for a minute, and the sensitive lips quivered, as she said, half under her breath,—

" But you are a man, and, pardon me, your very chivalry of gentleman makes you too lenient to a woman."

" Nay, I think a man can never be too lenient to a woman, Mrs Albany."

Her breast heaved, and her eyes filled, but she said nothing,—she dared not, he saw; and presently, with her exquisite womanly tact, turned the subject, as, fol-

lowing Harford ahead, she turned her horses
into Doring High Street, a wide irregular
mixture of shops and houses. Of course,
heads went round, or looked out of windows, and tongues wagged quickly enough
as the "young master" and his singular
companion drove past—he for the first time
since his accident,—and plentiful food was
gathered in for that queer meal which the
good ladies of a country town fondly
imagine is "five o'clock."

Talking now, and laughing too, in good-
natured amusement at "countryisms," the
two town-bred occupants of the carriage
drove on right through the market-place,
and so away again into the open country,
with ever-changing views of "hill and wold
and river," at every turn of the road, till at
length, on the summit of a hill, they could
see Luna Park, with its rich woods and
winding river, miles away behind them.

"How the road narrows here," Gabrielle
remarked presently. "It would be quite

impossible for two vehicles to pass here, would it not ? If one came round that turn ahead."

Douglas's answer was a laugh, and a hand pointing ahead as, round that very turn, came a dashing horse and trap, driven by a gentleman, with a page at his side.

All saw the situation in a moment. Harford stopped short. Mrs Albany drew up her spirited horses splendidly, and the gentleman, pulling up sharply, sprang to the ground and came up to the phaeton, lifting his hat to the handsome and very distingué looking occupants.

" I really must beg pardon," he began, and then the ludicrousness of the contretemps was irresistible. All three broke into a laugh, and even Harford gave vent to a respectfully smothered, decorous little sound.

" 'A regular fix,' " said Glen-Luna ; then, slightly raising himself from his half-reclining position amongst the cushions,

" what is to be done ? There is no siding for a long way, I think."

" I will back my trap to a gate just round the turn," said the stranger. " I am so sorry to keep a lady waiting."

" Pray, do not mention it," she answered, smiling ; " it will give the horses a rest."

" You are very kind to put it so, madam," said the stranger, glancing at the beautiful face as he stepped back. " I will be as quick as possible."

But Harford, who had dismounted, seeing that Gabrielle had the horses well in hand, threw his bridle over a bush bough in the hedge, and turned, touching his hat.

" I will help you, sir, if you will allow me."

" Thank you, very much ; but perhaps your master and mistress—"

Douglas's musical tones struck pleasantly across,—

" Will both be pleased for you to accept assistance in such a troublesome job. My horses are quite safe,"—adding, with an amused smile to Gabrielle, as the two men went off,—

"Handsome fellow, and looks clever. I wonder if he is the new doctor Jessie so recommended to your powers of captivation? Don't you feel tempted to try, Mrs Albany?"

She laughed, and answered lightly, with her expressive foreign shrug,—

"Ma foi, monsieur, I will not interfere with Jessie's fun."

"You certainly would prove a dangerous rival; I'm afraid little Jessie would not have a chance, pretty as she is."

"Why not? Some people prefer daisies and buttercups to exotics."

"Yes; some men do."

Clearly the speaker was not one of them.

"There is a frightful lot of humbug talked sometimes about it," he added. "Wild flowers are all very well in their place, but after all, they cannot compare to their cultivated brethren any more than their two prototypes in human nature can bear it. Why the wild flower should be more 'innocent' than the rarest black rose or richest tropic beauty of culture's own rearing, or the taste for the first be more pure than the love of the last I cannot see. God made them both. It is exactly the same cant as the school which talks of the desperate vice of town and the sweet innocence of the country. Bah! They should say 'ignorance' instead. I have not been a saint any more than my neighbours; I've knocked about half over the world—in towns and out of towns—and seen enough of the wickedness of both, and I never could find out that in any one way the cities were greater sinners; rather the other way, for country vice is coarse and ignorant, its crime both stupid and brutal—extra counts against the 'innocent purity' of rurality, I think."

"I thoroughly go with you, Mr Douglas,

both in opinion and experience, and mine has given me right enough to know." She added that half to herself with a smothered sigh, then looked up with a restless movement and a little laugh. "But how oddly we have strayed from Jessie and our stranger. Here comes Harford."

The courier came up, saluting.

"It's all right now, madam, if you'll please drive on slow and keep the off side of the road as much as you can."

He loosed his own horse, mounted, and rode forward, the carriage following to where the gentleman's trap stood, crushed close to a gate in the hedge, so as just to allow room, with care, for the phaeton to pass.

Courteous thanks and adieux were exchanged, and the two parties each went on their opposite ways.

"I believe I guess who that young fellow is," muttered the stranger, looking after the retreating carriage. I've heard of him already. What a cruel thing that such strength and perfect beauty should be laid low. It *can't* be hopeless. I wish I had charge of him, by heaven, if he were too poor to pay a pound! I do, as sure as my name is Chandos Neville!"

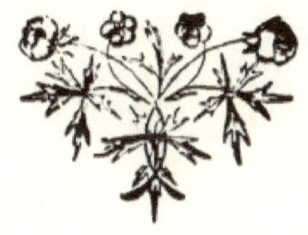

CHAPTER VIII.

IT'S NO BUSINESS OF MINE.

I REMEMBER once hearing recited a very clever serio-comic piece in verse, setting forth the manner in which a pair of country ladies, over their "dish" of tea, began by picking holes in the bonnet of a certain neighbour, and ended by entirely taking away her character.

I think that all these sort of coteries were invented by Lucifer as a happy thought to fill up all the odd corners of wickedness, just as the German toymakers, in packing their exporting boxes, fill up all the spaces and corners with those fascinating carved-wood animals made by the children of the Black Forest, which we all remember as the delight of our childish days.

Look at that coterie of Doring ladies, seated over afternoon tea—one can hardly call it by the fashionable name of "five o'clock"—on the pretty lawn of Mrs Winstanley's house, not far from the new doctor's residence. None of these fair ones were on visiting terms at the Hall, of course, but some happy few of them, the hostess for one, enjoyed the honour of a bowing acquaintance with "that sweet little thing," Lady Glen-Luna, who will often, if she meets them about, or sees them at their gate, stop her pony chair, and have a chat, when there is anything she wants passed about. But this is between ourselves; when she didn't care for that, the bright metallic treble would only cry out cheerily : "Ah, how do, dear Miss Chataway ? how's the school ? *such* a hurry, ta, ta."

But to-day, only about two hours after that carriage had driven through the little town, both my lady and her daughter had been seen to stop Mrs Winstanley in the market-place, and talk to her " for ever so long," no doubt all about this new inmate of the Hall, about whom all the tongues had wagged and surmised already, on such information as could be obtained from the back stairs.

" Saw them, my dear ? " said Miss Chataway, pursing up her lips, " of course I did, though he's never been out beyond the park before I believe, and yet, here, the very second day this ' secretary ' forsooth, comes, there they are right through the town, she driving, an' it please you,—nothing less than his own favourite blood horses will suit madam ; these foreigners are *so* impudent."

" Is she foreign ? " asked another lady, setting down her tiny teacup.

" She looks it, and has all that sort of manner, you know. My dear, depend upon

it, she's no stranger to monsieur, it's some
one he's known abroad."

"I daresay you are right, Miss Chataway.
I don't believe young Glen-Luna was a
saint," put in Mrs Orde, the wife of the
rival doctor to Mr Parker, who had never
been sent for to the Hall, "and I think
that her ladyship must be very—ahem !—
innocent to allow such a dashing, handsome
girl—"

Here Mrs Winstanley, big with superior
knowledge, turned round.

"My dear Mrs Orde, she is not so young
as she looks; Mrs Leicester Albany has
been married these nine years, ran away at
sixteen, and had to get a separation two
years ago. Lady Glen-Luna told me so
herself."

"Hum," said the doctor's wife, "I suppose, then, the truth is that she is a
divorcée. It's nonsense to pretend that any
woman who was at all particular would go
as secretary, or anything else, to a single

man. And if she is separated from her husband, depend upon it, it was her fault," Mrs Winstanley rejoined loftily.

"Dear Lady Glen-Luna quite knows what she is about, and, of course, would never have engaged a lady without—what she had—the highest references. Why," addressing another friend, "Mrs Albany was secretary and travelling companion to the late Professor Merton."

"Really," returned her friend, wisely, trying to look as if she knew perfectly well who Professor Merton was, "was she indeed? And he was—yes, of course—I see—"

"He was blind, you know; *so* clever," added Mrs Winstanley, who hadn't even heard the professor's name until that day, —"and thought very highly of the lady."

"Well, we shall see," said Miss Chataway sagaciously, "I don't like your separated wives. If matters go so far as that, why not have got a divorce at once and have done with it? It only looks as if she dared not! Don't it, Mrs Orde?"

"So I think, my dear, and my cook, who is cousin to the lodge-keeper at the park, told me that the family are going as usual for a month to London (Sir Arthur can't bear London longer), and, of course, this Mrs Albany will be left here with Mr Glen-Luna."

"Well, he must have some one, you see; and he's really an invalid, and she's a married woman," said Mrs Winstan-ley, sipping her tea, "and she's been in California, and is Bohemian, and doesn't care for these more civilised ideas, I suppose. It's not *my* business; and what sweet Lady Glen-Luna don't mind, I don't, I'm sure."

"I wonder she likes the responsibility of having such a charge when they're all away," said Mrs Orde viciously; and Mrs Winstanley replied urbanely,—

"Oh, but if he is taken ill, I daresay she

would send down at once for Dr Neville.
Are you going already?"

Of course she was; that last poke from
the rival leader in the very innocent faction
of the rural town was too much; and so
Mrs Doctor Orde took leave, and the party
soon after broke up, leaving Mrs Leicester
Albany's name much in the position of snow
just after very dirty hands have touched
it. It was well, and very natural, that the
woman who had suffered such danger to
honour itself was so superbly indifferent to
the petty gossip and scandal which bandied
her name, but could not touch herself. Poor
young thing!

CHAPTER IX.

A VERY STRANGE ACCIDENT.

"SO that is your adventure this morning, is it, brother mine? I saw them, too, pass here—the young lady driving."

A sweet gentle voice, that surely never spoke harshly of man, woman, or child; a broad, fair brow, and soft brown eyes, that could smile with the merry, or weep with the sorrowful, knowing what sorrow was; a white gentle hand, that had never drawn her robe from a fallen sister's touch, but rather been stretched out to save her; with quiet movements and noiseless garments, and silky tresses streaked with silver threads, coiled round the shapely head; and lips that only knew how to soothe and comfort—that was Rose Neville, of whom Leicester Albany's unhappy wife had said that day,—"I should like to know her,"—Chandos Neville's only and elder sister; so much older, indeed, for he was but five-and-thirty, that she had been sister and mother in one.

"Poor young fellow!" she added, sighing; "it made my heart ache to see him. I guessed it could only be Sir Arthur Glen-Luna's son, of whom we have heard, and his sister?"

"No, dear," Dr Neville answered; "for I actually asked, on my way home. She is a lady who has just come to be his secretary. She is married, they tell me; but separated from her husband."

"Poor young thing!" said pitying Rose; "it is a very painful and sad position for a woman so young and beautiful to be placed in. Not free, and yet utterly unprotected."

"I think the fellow who could be cruel to such a beautiful wife ought to be hanged!" said Chandos vigorously.

"Hush! dear boy," reproved Rose, smiling; "and did not Mr Parker or some one tell you that the young man was injured in a railway accident?"

"Ay! in saving a fellow passenger. Rose—"

"Well, dear?"

"Why, I wish etiquette was at Jericho, for I would give anything to try my hand with that young fellow! The old stationmaster has just been telling me about him. He says they've had all the crack physicians and surgeons—of course they have—but no one has got him beyond his present point; there is something in fault no one has yet reached, he says. Don't laugh at me, Rose; but I believe I'd find it out. I would take him in hand for nothing, if they'd let me; and if—well, of course, it's impossible, you know; and no doubt he's under the care of some big fish."

"I wish you could get the chance to try your skill, my dear. You are clever in all branches of your noble work; but if you have a *spécialité*, it is with spinal complaints. And I sometimes think, in your and many other callings, the younger blood brings fresher knowledge and bolder moves; less in a groove."

"Just so, Rose. Now, I suspect, for one thing, that young Glen-Luna has been kept too everlastingly reclining—reclining till he is worn and wearied to death, and the whole general health sinks and gradually gives way. He is colourless as a marble statue, and as delicately chiselled. He is a very slight-built man, I could see; but it's more than that. He is wasted; his features, his hands are as delicate as a woman's. Cut down like that at thirty! Heaven! it must be killing the man by inches! Rose, if I could have him for a patient, I would stake my whole reputation on this case."

" Darling Chandos ! how your enthusiasm does me good to see ! " said Rose, kissing the broad clear brow so like her own. " Surely your noble wish will be granted in some way."

" I don't know." He got up and began pacing to and fro the long room ; for it was after dinner, and they were in the drawing-room. " We seldom get our wishes, I think. Bah ! " said he, ruffling up his curly locks impatiently. " I'm a great fool, Rose. I cannot get that man's face or voice out of my head."

" Don't try, Chandos," said Miss Neville, with a quiet smile, as her eyes rested on the handsome, earnest face of the physician ; " for you are far too tender-hearted ever to grow callous or fail to feel, even suffer, in others' sufferings."

" I daresay you are right, Rose ; you

always are, dear.   Ha! what's that?   What
a peal at the bell!"

So there was, and some vehicle had
stopped at the gate.   The next moment
a man's voice at the door asked quickly if
Dr Neville was at home.

Chandos stepped out into the hall at
once, Rose behind him, catching a glimpse
over his shoulder of a groom in dark blue
and silver livery.

"I am Dr Neville.   Who wants me?"

"Mrs Albany, sir, up at Luna Hall, sent
me off with a trap to fetch you back to Mr
Glen-Luna.   There was an accident with
the lift, just at the top, and the master
hurt.   It would have been a much worse
jerk, sir, only Mrs Albany was beside his
chair on the lift, and the moment something broke, and it ran up too quick, she
throwed one arm round his shoulder to save
him from the danger, and with the other
caught the gallery rail, sir.   Then she and
Harford got the chair off, and lifted the

master on to a sofa in his dressing-room; and then he swooned dead off, sir, with the pain, for it shook him, you see, terrible. Mrs Albany just looked at me, and says, 'Fetch Dr Neville, Marston.'"

"I'll join you directly."

He vanished into his little surgery at the back for a few moments, and came back with a small valise.

"Good-bye, sister Rose. I am ready, Marston."

Chandos Neville only asked a few questions on the short drive.

"Where were Sir Arthur and the ladies?"

The groom answered that they had gone over to dine at Colonel Rosslyn's place, some ten miles off, and were not even expected back that night.

"You see, sir, it was like this," explained Marston, who was Douglas's own groom. "In the evening Mr Douglas and Mrs Albany (that is his new secretary) was out in the gardens, she pushing the chair, and

they came round to the stables, 'cause, sir,
he wanted to show her his Arab, Hassan,
that she's to ride. Well, sir, after they'd
gone back to the west wing, where his
rooms and hers are, you know, I picked up
a beautiful gold brooch I had noticed in her
lace kerchief. So I just took it round myself
to give her, and when I stepped into the
west hall door, there was Harford at the top
working up the lift, and *they* in it. I ran up
the stairs, and had got up beside Harford
(that's Mr Douglas's courier, sir), when the
lift came half way to the level, and then
something below gave way, as I said, and
up it ran awful. It's a good chance I was
there, too, because I took the gear from Harford and held the lift as Mrs Albany stopped
it, and Harford helped Mrs Albany—who is,
sir, the greatest brick!" said the groom enthusiastically, "if you'll pardon me. Most
women would ha' screamed, and never held
him as she did ; but though she went as
white as death—for I'm sure in that hor-

rible minute we all thought the whole thing
was going to rush up and smash them both
to death — she never moved a muscle or
flinched one hair's-breadth. And strong—
Lord, sir, she *is* wonderful nerve and strength
for a woman! To see how she gripped the
chair! And I verily believe that if Will
Harford hadn't been there, she'd ha' man-
aged to lift him on to the sofa all herself."

"She looks that sort of brave woman,"
said the physician. "I met them out
this morning. Ah, here we are, thank
Heaven!"

Another servant was at the open west
wing door, under orders, on the look-out,
and at once conducted the welcome, anxiously
looked-for visitant up to the floor above,
and to the door of the *salon*, where Harford,
hearing steps, met them, with a glad look
of recognition and deep-breathed "Thank
God! you're come, sir!"

And he led him into the elegant dressing-
room. There, on a wide, low couch, lay

that graceful form, the beautiful head lying on Gabrielle's left arm, as she knelt beside him, her own firm, steadfast face scarcely less deathly than the one over which she bent, as she kept softly passing the right hand, wet with fragrant eau de Cologne, over temples and brow and round the lips, wetting even the silky moustache that shaded them.

"An invaluable nurse, I can see!" said the relieved doctor, stooping down to listen to the sufferer's breathing. "Has he revived or spoken at all, Mrs Albany?"

"We got him round a little after the first painful agony had done its work," she answered quietly; "but he was not fully conscious, for the only word he spoke audibly showed that he took me for his own dead mother. Then he relapsed again, I think from sheer exhaustion. His teeth were set, his hands clenched with agony, when he swooned. I don't think he is entirely unconscious."

The physician took up one of those slender

hands in his own soft palm, and laid one finger on the wrist; then shook his head, and turned to his valise.

"Yes," he said; "we must get back full consciousness before I can see what mischief is done. A little water in that small wine glass, please, Harford."

Harford obeyed gladly, and held the glass for Neville, while he produced a vial from his case, and dropped some of its contents into the water."

"Thanks! Raise his head higher, please, Mrs Albany."

She simply lifted it from her arm to her bosom.

"Try if he knows your voice enough to drink this."

In the same quiet way, like one resolutely suppressing intense feeling, she took the glass and held it to the bloodless lips, bending her head lower as she deliberately made use of the illusion she had mentioned.

" Drink this, Douglas, for your mother's sake ! "

Closed, indeed, must be the ear into which that low, pathetic voice of tender music could not penetrate, winged with the one sacred name of a thousand halos, to which no agony, mental or physical, can ever entirely deafen the ear or numb the heart —" Mother ! " The heavily-fringed eyelids quivered, the lips parted a little as the glass touched them ; in a minute she gave Chandos back the empty glass.

" You are a magician ! " he said, smiling. " Keep him as he is, please ; unless you are tired."

She glanced keenly up in the fine face, with its bright, full, hazel eyes, and sweet, firm mouth, and half smiled.

" I should not be wearied, if you wished me to keep your patient like this all night. I am a tireless nurse."

" I believe *that*," said Neville, and then stood with folded arms, watching in anxious

silence for the effect of the powerful re-
storative he had administered. Only a few
moments of such suspense, and then a sharp
shiver went through the whole frame, and
one hand was moved restlessly, as if seek-
ing something. Gabrielle laid hers in it at
once, and his fingers closed round it closely,
with a long-drawn breath over the lips,
which, if faint, was still one of relief; still
half unconscious, he knew at least that that
was the touch he sought.

"Is she—safe? O God! Not killed—
to save me!" The dark eyes opened
suddenly, with an almost wild look of
horror. "I thought—and then that awful
agony—"

If that beautiful woman's heart ached and
throbbed with bitter, sudden pain, dull and
vague, who knew it but herself as she said
softly,—

"Hush, I am safe. You are resting
against me now, and holding my hand—
Gabrielle Albany."

"Ah!—it is her voice—or—my mother's —she called me just now—"

Dr Neville took up a bottle of salts, and bent down, holding it cautiously, just within inhaling distance. A fear possessed him that the physical shock and agony had possibly not let the sensitive brain escape quite unscathed.

"Are you in pain now? Some pillows, Harford, please."

There was no answer to the question, but there was a start at the strange voice, gentle as it was—probably what the clever doctor meant. He waited a moment until the pillows were placed to his liking, and then said, smiling,—

"Now, nurse, lay him back."

"It will disturb him, Dr Neville, if I loose my left hand; he has it so tight."

"Exactly what I want; he must be roused."

"Eh bien, monsieur."

She drew her hand free with some difficulty, and gently laid him against the pillows, laying her hand on his brow a moment.

The movement, the touch, had the desired effect, for he started again, shivered and opened his eyes, once more with a strange look that, going from face to face, half puzzled and pained, a gradual recognition growing slowly, as it came back to hers with a sweet, restful look that made Chandos draw a deep breath of relief.

"Ah, forgive; I am not worth such trouble."

"You know your nurse, then?" said the physician brightly.

A moment's pause, but the hand sought and clasped hers again; then the low, languid tones answered,—

"Yes, oh yes; and Harford—"

"Not me yet, eh?"

The drooping lids and sweeping lashes were lifted a moment.

"Yes, we met you—to-day."

"Right; I am Dr Neville. Are you in pain now?"

"Not much."

"A dull aching?" said Chandos, who had to an extraordinary degree that rare and invaluable gift to the physician of exactly hitting upon the patient's suffering, "such as comes after a fearful wrench?"

"Yes."

"Drink this before we go further."

He mixed a little brandy and water in the wine-glass and gave it to Gabrielle.

Douglas drank it. He only knew the fierce agony he had suffered, though perhaps both tender nurse and physician could nearly gauge it by the force of the almost instant deadly swoon and frightful exhaustion following. As Gabrielle replaced the empty glass, Neville said, in a low tone,—

"I will see now, Mrs Albany, whether this accident has done more than cause cruel pain and exhaust strength, if you will kindly wait in the next room till I come or call you. Your courage and promptness has saved him."

The colour flushed her cheek for a moment, but she only bowed her head and glided away, closing the door between the two apartments. As she passed Harford, Dr Neville saw the two exchange a look that puzzled and haunted him long afterwards. What could it mean?

CHAPTER X.

SISTER ROSE'S WORDS COME TRUE.

WHEN Chandos Neville came out into the *salon*, Mrs Albany was standing by the furthest window, in the full flood of moonlight, her hands locked loosely before her; her face, with all its world of passion and power beneath the statuesque surface, half uplifted, the great dark eyes looking out with a far-off gaze that saw only the gloom and shadows of her ill-starred life—perhaps already the deeper, darkest misery of all that was creeping slow and deathlike upon her! But the whole attitude and expression of face and form struck him very painfully. So young still—looking almost a girl—what had been her life, her marriage? had she ever cared for the husband from whom she was separated?

"Well," she said, turning quickly to him, with an instant change of the mobile face, "what is your opinion?"

"That your prompt action has saved him from at least being crippled for life, Mrs Albany. That, after a very close and careful examination, I am satisfied that no further permanent injury has been added to that originally done by the railway accident; and a few days' care and rest will restore him to his usual strength."

"Thank God."

She turned aside abruptly for a minute, pressing her small hands on her heaving breast, almost giving way in the sudden relief from deadly suspense; shaken, too, herself more than she thought by the shock and strain on her strength, as the physician saw.

"You need some care yourself," he said quietly; but she interrupted him.

"No, no! Hush! Not me! Tell me what you wish done for him."

"He must not be moved from where he is till I come to-morrow morning. He has on his *robe de chambre* now, and will do very well for the night. I hope he will sleep quietly. There is no need for either you or Harford to sit up; but if he will sleep in the dressing-room too, and you somewhere within easy call—"

"My apartments are just opposite these," she interposed; "and there is bell communication between all these rooms and mine and the courier's, and I am a very light sleeper. But let me sit up in here."

"Certainly not! I do not at all think he will swoon again, or have any return of that frightful agony or exhaustion consequent upon it; but if there is, give him, yourself, a repetition of the dose you saw me give."

" You will come up early, Dr Neville ? "

" I will, indeed. I will remain here all night if you wish it, Mrs Albany."

" You are too kind ! No ; not as you think it unnecessary. I suppose you know about the accident ? "

" From Harford ; yes. Poor young fellow ! It would be the greatest happiness—" He stopped ; bit his lip, and almost abruptly held out his hand. " Goodnight, then, Mrs Albany."

But, instead of giving him her hand, she laid it on his arm detaining him.

" Pardon me ! " she said steadily. " I have been watching you and taking note ever since you came. I had heard that you were very clever, and I fully believe it. Dr Neville, I am going to speak plainly in the very strongest interest of that man lying in that room, and I entreat you to answer me as plainly—setting aside all motives of professional etiquette and delicacy which would usually hold you silent, as absolutely as I do ; all those considerations and fears of the world which would make most women shrink from the position I hold here, and which I do not intend to resign unless Mr Glen-Luna himself, in whose service I am, wishes it."

"Mrs Albany, I admire your moral courage as I do your physical bravery," said Chandos warmly. "Speak as you will ; I will answer if I can."

"Thank you ! Well, it needs hardly to tell you that no expense has been spared on Sir Arthur's only son ; no science left untried ; and yet he is still no further than you see. There is something that none of your faculty have quite mastered in this case. They admit it. They have kept him more or less lying down — the mind restless, fretted—a physician must know the whole truth. Left cruelly to himself, when he should have had at least one tender, devoted companion—it has acted on the physique, and the general strength and health have suffered." The physician stood now with very grave brow and downcast eyes, listening intently. "The great and very experienced in any profession sometimes fall into grooves where the younger, more vigorous blood strikes out some bolder path or more daring venture. You start!"

"Pardon me—did I? My sister's very words to-night, when we were speaking of Mr Glen-Luna."

"Ha! you were?—and the answer you gave her—"

"Mrs Albany!" Chandos Neville flushed to his brow and drew back a step, but she laid both her hands on his with a grasp more like a man's than a woman's.

"Dr Neville, if you think, from your examination just now, that you can make Douglas Glen-Luna what he was, in heaven's name speak out, and on me be the charge."

The passionate force of the woman, that in its grand earnestness absolutely flung aside self and what he might think, bore all hesitation on his part before it, and made it even seem to him cowardice before her courage.   He looked up, his eyes aglow.

" Mrs Albany, forgive me ; you shame me.   Under heaven, I believe I *can* restore him to all the perfect beauty and strength which that heaven gave him !   I believe I have found the very seat of the injury done, which has been hitherto missed, and I dare now repeat emphatically to you and him—the answer I gave my sister this evening—I will willingly stake my whole reputation on this case."

He so flung the power of his own conviction into her, as some doctors do, it was so much more than she had dared to hope, that she gave way for a moment, and covered her face.

When she faced him again, the long lashes were still wet ; the dark eyes met his with almost an appealing look that touched him.

" Forgive my weakness.   I have only

been two days under this roof. I am nothing but his paid servant as much as Harford
—less, indeed, for he has served his master
for years, I only hours, and yet—"

"Nay—yet—you are nurse and he—
patient, helpless," said Chandos quietly.

"Ay, that is it. I am only a woman,
Dr Neville," with a faint smile, "and it
made my very heart ache to see a young
strong man cut down, laid low; wrecked for
life, dependent for so much on others—on
me—helpless. I thought till I came here
that I had grown hard, as well as reckless
of the world."

She paused a moment, and then added,
regaining her usual manner with an effort,—

"What I say I know he himself will
ratify to-morrow, and to Sir Arthur all
his son does is right! From this hour,
Dr Neville, that son is in your hands."

He bowed gravely over the hand he held,
and touched his lips to it.

"Till to-morrow, then, Mrs Albany, *au*

revoir. No, do not ring for a servant; I know my way just down to that hall."

"Marston is waiting there to drive you home, but—ah, here comes Harford."

As Chandos Neville went out, the courier came in.

"Would you mind stepping in to Mr Douglas, madam, for he asked me just now —as I thought he was going off so nicely— —whether I was quite sure you weren't injured."

"I was just going in for a minute, Harford. Just show Dr Neville down to the dog-cart, and come back here."

Chandos followed Harford, Gabrielle passed noiselessly into the dressing-room, with its lowered lights, and soft summer air fanning in, laden with the mingled scent of flowers and eau de Cologne.

Douglas was lying so still, with averted face, that she almost hoped he slept, but no; the head was turned languidly to her, with a faint, glad smile on the lips, and in the wide open, tired eyes that looked up into hers as she bent over him.

"Now, you see that I am quite unhurt, and you must try to sleep; you are worn out."

"I am tired; oh, so tired! I think, perhaps, too weary to sleep."

"Then see, I must try what my art as nurse can do. Does your head ache?"

"A little."

She perfectly wetted both her hands with the cool essence of Cologne, and once more kneeling down beside him, laid one hand in his, and kept passing the other slowly, lightly across the broad brow, and under the rich bronze locks that curled so thickly above it. Did she know then, or did he, the magic of her touch, her presence? Ah me, no, it was felt, not seen, subtle, intangible, unrecognised, but there already as surely as the blue sea tosses, and knows not its own passionate surging depths. The painful wakefulness of over-weariness was fain forced to yield to such a spell of might as this, and the patient nurse, the tender woman, had her reward soon ; the dark eyes closed, the chiselled lips settled restfully, the fingers that had closed over hers relaxed, and he lay asleep, just breathing softly in all the unconscious grace and beauty of a most perfect statue—but a statue endowed with the marvellous gift of life and immortality.

Then she softly stole away into the next room, carefully closing the door of communication.

William Harford was standing there, waiting for her, and for a minute each faced the other with the same look that had so puzzled Chandos Neville. Each perfectly understood the other, but neither chose to put thought or suspicion into precise words, though the man spoke first.

" Mrs Albany, if that gear, *wherever the fault in it was*, had given way entirely, both

you and the master would have been dashed
to pieces against the roof."

"I know that, Harford."

It hardly seemed the same voice and face
that had spoken, and bent so soothingly, so
tenderly, with such sweet womanliness, to
the sleeper in the next room ; so stern and
set voice and face now, as the few words
fell that to him said such a volume.

"I know it, Harford."

"I have telegraphed already to the man
in town who made this," added the courier,
"to come at once and put entirely new gear
to the lift, and the same extraordinary accident will not occur again. *You* know, I
suppose, Mrs Albany "—the man asked this
abruptly—"who is the next heir or successor
to the master ?"

"I never heard yet," said Gabrielle
slowly.

"You can guess !"

"Yes."

"Will you say, Mrs Albany ?"

" No."

" Shall I tell you ? "

" If you like."

" Lady Glen-Luna's daughter, Jessica."

She made no answer to that, only stood looking at him. He spoke again in another tone.

" Mrs Albany, you won't leave Mr Douglas, will you ? '

" Leave! certainly not ; why should I, unless he himself dismisses me ? "

" He'll never do that, madam ; but," the man moved uneasily now, and dropped his keen eyes, "pardon me ; I'm a man over forty, and you are married, or I shouldn't venture—"

" Go on, good, faithful Harford."

" Well, ma'am, you see—those detestable village gossips will talk of you being here, you know, and pull you to pieces—most ladies in your place would take fright and go."

" I shall not, Harford, if they said the

very worst that scandal can invent," said Albany's wife calmly,—" not because I hold my name lightly, or am hard, or over reckless, but because, even if no interest kept me here, I despise village doings too utterly to care what they say; they are nothing to me. And there is every interest to keep me here; we are one. Are you satisfied?"

" Quite, thank you, Mrs Albany."

No more was said; they parted in silence—those two who were in Douglas Glen-Luna's service—and so the night of that terrible day ended.

CHAPTER XI.

BEHOLD, A LITTLE CLOUD ARISETH NOW,
LIKE UNTO A MAN'S HAND.

IT is very rarely in this life that our most earnest hopes are fulfilled, our dearest wishes realised. I suppose because our finite humanity, only "seeing through a glass darkly," too often yearns for that which our all-seeing Creator knows is not for our highest good. *Quem Deus amat castigat.* But sometimes, though it so falls to very few, the very thing which though wished for, seemed most absolutely beyond reach, rises up before us—not a chimæra or wild dream—but a fact, a reality, actually in our grasp. So it was now with

Chandos Neville, and it calls for no very unusually dramatic or sympathetic nature to understand, or sympathise with, the even passionate joy of a man whose whole high earnest soul and large-hearted nature were in his noble profession, who suddenly finds his greatest, yet most hopeless, wish gained.

The lights still shone from the dining-room windows when he reached home, and his sister was sitting up for him.

" Rose ! You naughty Sister Rose."

" I was too anxious to sleep, dear, but your face tells me good news—some more than usual news," she added, as the bright gas-light fell full on his face.

He put both arms round his sister, and dropped his head on her shoulder. The strong man was trembling like a child.

" Oh, Rose, I am so happy ! my wish is granted."

" Thank God !"

Beyond the fervent reverence of those two words no other passed her lips till, after a few minutes' stillness, he lifted himself, with one deep-drawn breath, and drew back.

" You always know how I feel, Rose, and feel with me."

Chandos drew her to her arm-chair again, and, seating himself on one of its arms, said,—

" You remember what we were talking of this evening, Sister Rose ? "

" Yes, my dear."

" Rose, Douglas Glen-Luna is my patient henceforth ; Mrs Albany has placed him absolutely in my hands.   Ah! I tell you that woman is a heroine, in the fullest, grandest sense of the word."

" Tell me all about it, Chandos."

She listened with the silence of deepest interest to his account of his new patient and his attendant, and the accident which had been so nearly a terribly fatal one to both.

Oddly enough her words, as he concluded,

were exactly those Gabrielle had said of her
—" I should like to know her."

The ormolu clock struck one as she spoke,
and she rose up.

" See, dear; it is time we both retired.
How early shall you drive over to the
Hall ?"

" About nine o'clock," Dr Neville answered, bolting up shutter and door. " I
wonder how the accident happened ; it
was so very extraordinary."

" Did not Mrs Albany or the courier seem
to know ?" asked Miss Neville, as the two
went upstairs together.

" I don't think so," said Chandos slowly,
" but I am puzzled. I have a queer fancy.
I saw such an odd look pass between those
two. I think they have some suspicion
resting somewhere."

" Perhaps one of the servants has been
meddling with the lift."

" It may be ; if any one has, they must
have felt pleasant when it gave way with

those two lives upon it," said the doctor dryly. "Good night, Rose."

He kissed his sister, and turned into his room ; and his dreams were a strange jumble of broken lifts, and some one stopping him in a lane to fetch him to save some one from being murdered, and when he went he found himself amidst a thick darkness, and a crowd surging wildly to and fro, crying out where, in Heaven's name, were Douglas Glen-Luna and Gabrielle. And then there came a heavy knocking somewhere, which woke the dreamer with a start—and, lo! the house-maid was tapping at the door, and telling him it was half-past seven, and his hot-water was outside.

An hour and a-half later, the physician's pretty brougham—for he kept one besides his trap—drew up at the west wing door of Luna Hall, and he was at once admitted.

"Thanks! I know the way," he said, as the servant was about to precede him ; and up the wide staircase he went, two at a

time, through the *salon*, and tapped at the
dressing-room door.

"Come in!" said Gabrielle's soft voice,
and as he entered she met him with a glad
smile and warm hand-clasp of welcome.

Douglas was lying back on the couch,
from which, according to orders, he yet had
not been stirred; his head turned a little
aside, his eyes closed — too prostrate, it
seemed, for even a movement of restlessness. But it was evident every sense was
keenly alive, for the moment Neville entered the head turned, and it was good to
see the bright light of pleasure that banished
the languor from the beautiful grey eyes, as
the hand was stretched out. Surely there
is something much to sweeten the anxious
care and often terrible responsibility of the
medical profession, especially to such a man
as Chandos Neville; and he is no fancy or
very unusual a picture either.

"You look much too colourless and languid," he said, smiling: and his smile, like

his whole manner, was gentle, cheering, bright yet mellowed—a man whose mere presence in a sick-room seemed to bring light and relief to both nurse and patient. "How have you slept?"

"Well enough, thank you! I am better."

"What does nurse say?"

The dark eyes turned on her with such a look, and then a heavy sigh.

"Ah! sweet nurse! What a trouble and anxiety I am to you all!"

Her soft fingers were laid on his lips, with the sweet, chiding tenderness with which we touch a child.

"Hush, or I shall scold you! May we move him at all, Dr Neville? Ah! pardon; you cannot tell yet. I will send Harford to you, and you will find me in the next room."

Mrs Albany rang the bell, and passed out as Harford was entering from the corridor.

"Madam, Mr Boyd himself has just come to see to the lift. Will you see him yourself?"

" Yes, Harford, while you attend to Mr
Douglas. Is Mr Boyd in the hall ? "

" Yes, madam ; with one of his men."

" *C'est bien !* We shall take care no
such accident happens again ! " she said
in French, and went downstairs.

" Good morning, madam ! I hope I am
not too early," began Mr Boyd, wondering
who this handsome lady was ; " but the
telegram was so urgent, that I thought I
had better take the last train down over
night, and stop in Doring."

" Quite right. I am obliged to you for
your prompt answer to my summons. A
most unaccountable and nearly fatal accident happened to the lift last evening while
Mr Glen-Luna and myself were ascending
by it ; for as we came half way up to
the gallery something in the gear below
suddenly gave way, and the lift ran
up. When did you last examine this
machine ? "

" Only one month ago, madam ; my own

self, because naturally Sir Arthur is so particular over it."

" Well, and was it then sound ? "

" As sound as a bell, madam ! I will swear that, if it was my last word. Why, ma'am, the whole thing was put up new only a year ago, and as perfect as skill and money could make it. Sir Arthur spared no expense, and we no skill. Why, all the chains and gear was made double strong ! If I didn't see the thing there, I'd never have believed it could have happened like this. I can't make it out."

" Nor I ! " said Mrs Albany quietly. " Look at the machinery, and tell me what the mischief is, if you can."

She stood by while the two men bent down, watching them, as motionless as a statue, save for the quick, short heave of her breast beneath the firm, delicate hands folded over it.

So watching, she saw the two men suddenly look at each other, each with a quick, low " Whew—w— "

"Well?" said Gabrielle Albany, as Mr Boyd was erect again.

"It's just this, madam. The machinery has been damaged in some unaccountable way — perhaps roughly used. It is not safe now; it don't need to be a mechanic to see this."

"It is most extraordinary!" she said; "but of course Sir Arthur will sift it to the bottom when he returns. Meanwhile, Mr Glen-Luna wishes you to thoroughly examine the whole machine, lest there may be any other damage done. If you consider it in the least necessary, or even advisable, the whole thing must come down and be refitted. I am Mr Glen-Luna's secretary, and fully empowered to give you orders."

Mr Boyd bowed very low, and Gabrielle returned to the *salon*, leaving them to their work of inspection.

Dr Neville was waiting for her.

"I am still of the same opinion, Mrs Albany. There is no further permanent injury done, and I think, with a few days of care and quiet, we shall get rid of the prostration consequent on the shock and agony he suffered. Keep away everything and every one that can fret him. I want both body and that tiresome, restless brain of his kept perfectly quiet, for to-day at any rate ; and if"—Chandos smiled—" you can by any arts witch him into sleep presently, pray do."

" No one shall come near him but myself and Harford, Dr Neville," said Gabrielle firmly ; " and you will call in again to-day ? "

" Certainly—this evening."

" And of course I am not to tell him what passed between us last night, until he has recovered his strength ? "

" I must leave that a good deal to your, I know, unerring judgment, Mrs Albany ; for if you find him fretting about that very thing, as is very likely, tell him what you think best."

"You shall be obeyed like a veritable autocrat," she said, smiling a little. "I shall not leave him except for a few minutes even when the family come home. Ah! what is this?"

A footman with a telegram.

"For you, if you please, madam," he said, and withdrew.

"One moment, Dr Neville. Ah, thank Heaven, they are not coming back till Monday. Read."

It was from Lady Glen-Luna, to say that the Rosslyns would not hear of their return till Monday (this being Saturday).

"The best thing that could possibly have happened," said Chandos. "We shall have our charge driving out again by then, I hope. Good-bye till evening, Mrs Albany."

He shook hands and vanished just as Harford entered. Gabrielle gave him the telegram.

"I am more glad than I can say, Mrs Albany; though, of course, you would not have allowed them to see the master.   And about the lift, madam ? "

" Harford, Boyd's positive opinion confirms our worst suspicions."

The man looked up, and their eyes met.

" You mean," he said, under his breath, and put one hand on her arm, " that it is true beyond doubt that the *machinery has been tampered with ?* "

" Yes."

They stood facing each other in dead silence, which neither broke for some seconds.   Then the courier dropped his hand, and said slowly,—

" We understand each other perfectly then, Mrs Albany ? "

" Yes—perfectly, Harford."

The man went through the ante-room ; the woman passed as noiselessly into the dressing-room, and paused beside the couch on which that stricken, prostrate form of beauty lay.

Hearts feel that love thee !—hearts feel that love thee ! Ah, me, for the little cloud that ariseth like unto a man's hand !

CHAPTER XII.

GIVING A DIAMOND.

GABRIELLE paused beside that couch; bent over the helpless form, and said quietly,—

"They are not coming back till Monday."

A quick-drawn breath, an instant look of intense relief in the dark, tired eyes that met hers.

"I am so glad! But you would not have let them come up?"

"No! You are to be kept very quiet to-day, and see no one."

"Except my dear nurse! They mean it all kindly," Douglas added, as if in explanation; "but they make such a fuss. You know what I mean. I am absurd, over-sensitive, morbid; but, still—"

Still, still, he was a man; and the very pride of his manhood, that glories in its rich strength, shrank in horrible dread from notice and effusive pity in his sufferings, even when it was sincere. His stepmother and sister at all times jarred on every chord of the finely-attuned instrument, and now every sensitive nerve had been quivering at the mere thought of their coming near him; while this woman, who had come into his crushed, hopeless life like a strain of most wondrous music, soothed by her mere presence.

"Still!" Gabrielle repeated, laying her cool hand on his brow. "I perfectly understand you; but you must give this brain rest, and not think."

"Not think!" he said. "Not *think!* of what I was, and what I am—of the living death that all my future will be. My God! but for your precious life I wish the lift had crashed to the bottom, and dashed me to pieces."

"Hush! Oh, hush!" It so wrung her heart, that only the strongest mastery of a strong will forced back the tide of emotion that for one second had almost broken down self-control, as she knelt down at his side, clasping his hand with hands that trembled. "I cannot bear that from you, when—"

"Forgive me, dear Mrs Albany! Forgive me such a selfish outburst of misery! I am weak, unmanned to-day, I think. I forgot myself quite. I am beaten down utterly in spirits!"

"Hush! Listen to me!" said Gabrielle, with one imperative hand on his lips for a minute. "I see that it is best to give you something happier to think of, since I cannot arrest thought, even by sleep."

Douglas turned his head sharply, so as to bring his searching gaze full on her face; and his hand closed almost convulsively on hers, as she still knelt.

"You will have to forgive me beforehand," she said, smiling now, though her lips quivered, "for taking a liberty with your name, and pledging you to ratify something I have done."

"It can only be right if you did it, whatever it is."

"My pardon is signed, sealed, and delivered then, Mr Douglas. Well," she laid one hand now on his shoulder, fearful lest he should start half up or make some sudden movement at her words; "I spoke to Dr Neville last night, and he thinks there is some hope for you!"

The blood rushed to Douglas's bronzed cheeks, and she felt him quiver under her hand; but the next minute he was deathly pale again, and shook his head.

"No, no! They have all said that at first, Mrs Albany."

"There is!" she said steadily. "I forced him to throw aside the professional etiquette that held him silent, and answer plainly my question whether he thought, from his recent examination, that he could do you any good. I will give you his answer, in his own more than earnest words. 'Under Heaven, I believe I can restore him to all the perfect strength which that Heaven gave him. I believe I have found the very seat of the injury done, which has hitherto been missed; and I dare now repeat emphatically what I said to my sister —that I will willingly stake my whole reputation on this case!'"

"O God!"

Such a dazzling blaze of glorious sunlight in the darkness, such a rush of mighty waters over the arid land, that manhood's proudest barriers gave way, and the man suddenly buried his face in the cushions with such a deep, passionate burst of emotion, as laid all check or control powerless for many seconds; and Gabrielle neither spoke nor moved till the soft voice came brokenly.

"Forgive my weakness. I try you so cruelly. I, who owe you life, and now—hope!"

"Hush, hush! You owe me nothing," she said, and quietly lifted his head to turn the cushions. "There now, you must keep very quiet," and, patting the curling locks, with a smile, "be my own good boy, or the poor nurse will fear she has done wrong to tell you."

"Ah! no, no, dear, sweetest nurse! And now you have not told me what it is I have to ratify?"

Exhausted he might be, physically; but she saw that she had done wisely to put even slight hope for despair, sweet for bitter, light for darkness.

"Only this, Mr Douglas. I told Dr Neville that from that minute you were entirely in his hands."

"Thank you."

He drew her hand to his lips, and kissed it with deep chivalrous reverence; then closed his eyes, saying quietly that he was very tired, and would try to sleep, because she wished it.

When Chandos Neville called in the evening he found his new patient markedly better and stronger, though still languid, and he asked Mrs Albany how soon the lift would be in order. She told him that an entirely new one from Mr Boyd's factory was to be sent on Monday, and fixed with some extra strong machinery.

"Which I told her was quite unnecessary," said Douglas, smiling; "for Boyd says that this one is sound, he believes, but she and Harford have put their heads together, and don't care one bit what I say."

"I may be over fanciful," said Gabrielle, "but it is a fault on the right side. I would never again see you in *this* lift without fear and dread of some other undiscovered damage."

Both men looked at her, both vaguely

struck by something in her voice of which perhaps she was scarcely conscious ; but she smiled brightly the next moment, and turned the subject.

"You have not yet ratified my words, Mr Douglas, so I'll leave you to do so."

And, putting down the book she had been reading to him when Neville entered, she went out of the room.

A new lift would, she felt sure, make all safe in that quarter. She had not much fear of a second "accident" with the machine. It would look too suspicious, and be fraught with too much danger to the hand that wrought the evil.

It is a terrible thing to have a venomous serpent at the very hearth.

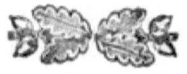

CHAPTER XIII.

SUNDAY MORNING.

DEAR me! how all Doring talked and gossiped over the new doctor and new secretary, and the accident at the Hall, even as it dressed and walked to church or meeting-house that Sunday. Of course it knew for a positive fact, my dear, everything that had (not) happened, and could state on the authority of everybody (not) concerned every word that could not possibly have been uttered. The poor little wee bits of truth that looked out might have cried out like the lamp-posts in our streets, " Where are you ?— Here am I ! " They knew that "that Mrs Albany" had sent off, post haste, for the swell London doctor, who had, after all, only come for a few months, while Mr Parker was away, and in consequence Mrs Doctor Orde went to church in a state of bitter piety that made her feel with intense morality that *she* was a straightforward, plain (as she was, heaven knows) married woman, and Mrs Leicester Albany! nobody knew what!

Gossip wondered that Sunday morning whether either she or "those Nevilles" would show in church at all. Of course they would at St Agnes the Martyr. The Hall was High Church from time immemorial, and of course they would do in Turkey as the Turkeys did; though no doubt the London doctor was an infidel, soaked with modern scientific unbeliefs, and "that foreigner"—a Papist—if, indeed, she was anything at all.

So those of the coterie who, like Mrs Doctor Orde, were evangelical, sailed into

their pews at St Luke's in all the agonies
of ignorance for two hours, even as to what
sort of bonnet or hat the new comer would
wear, and the worst suspicions that Mrs
Winstanley and some others would know
that important point before they could do
so, which was the fact, for Mrs W., passing
down the aisle, saw Mrs Albany still kneeling in nearly the last rows of chairs, and,
dear me ! she wore the very same dark
silk dress and dashing plumed hat in which
she had driven through the town on Friday.
And outside, at the churchyard gate (for
St Agnes's was the beautiful old parish
church) actually stood a dainty victoria in
charge of Mr Glen-Luna's own man, Marston. Upon my word ! Was madam too
grand to walk back across the park ? And
there was Dr Neville, too—waiting for her,
of course—though he had ridden up to the
Hall early that day; the gardener's boy had
seen him. Mrs Winstanley's eye is upon
them while she affects to be waiting about

for Mrs Orde to pass. Ah! the doctor's
face lights up—he sees her—no, it is only
his sister who joins him ; but, almost as
he stops, the tall, graceful figure followed
—came up, as they evidently waited for
her, and the doctor, lifting · his hat, with
a sort of *sans cérémonie* introduction,—

"My sister Rose is so anxious to know
you, Mrs Albany, that we have waited to
catch you."

"I am very much honoured, Miss Neville,"
the rich, low voice answers ; "and I assure
you the anxiety was reciprocal, for we saw
you as we drove by on Friday."

(" *We*, indeed," mutters Mrs W., with a
toss, "upon my word ; quite an adven-
turess.")

"Did you ?—I saw you. Will you walk
just back with us, and come in to luncheon ? "

"Thank you, Miss Neville ; you are very
kind, and I will walk back to your gate
with pleasure ; but I cannot, I think, leave
Mr Glen-Luna so much longer alone. He

insisted on my coming to church, as he was so much better. Marston ? "

" Yes, madam."

The groom touched his hat, and waited her orders, as if she had been his master, or a duchess at least.

" Will you just drive on to Dr Neville's gate, and wait for me there ? "

Marston saluted again, and drove off his pretty little horses, while his *pro tem.* mistress took the doctor's offered arm, and passed on between him and Sister Rose.

" I suspect," she said, smiling, " that my brother, although a good Tory, meditates a considerable revolution in the medical treatment of your charge, Mrs Albany."

" I think it is needed, Miss Neville, and I am very certain that I mean to make an entire revolution in his social treatment, subject, of course "—with an arch glance at Chandos—" to physician's autocracy. I am too true blue to defy legal authority."

" I think we shall find ourselves quite at

one, Mrs Albany ; and I have no fear that
you will allow the least interference with
your authority in Mr Glen-Luna's *ménage*,"
said the doctor, with a comical look in the
fine lines of the resolute mouth and brow.
Indeed, where was there a weak line at that
beautiful face, in which character was so
marked ?

"Certainly not. I could not take
such a responsibility without adequate
authority ! "

"Quite right, Mrs Nurse, and I am very
certain that Mr Glen-Luna will entirely
support you. Of Sir Arthur I know nothing. Do they know anything of this
accident, if I may ask ? "

"I wrote last night to Sir Arthur just to
say there had been a slight accident, that I
had called you in, and all was well with
his son, who, I added, had placed himself at once entirely under your medical
care."

"Thank you, Mrs Albany. I am glad

you have done so, and, God knows, I hope I shall justify the confidence you and Mr Glen-Luna have reposed in me."

" I am sure of one thing, Dr Neville, that if you fail, it will not be from any fault of yours."

He bowed gravely, and Miss Neville asked if they had discovered the cause of the accident.

" Some flaw in the chain, I believe," Gabrielle answered ; " but a new lift is to be put up on Monday. I felt quite safe, you see, in acting without the least regard to expense, for Sir Arthur would sooner lose half his fortune than have any risk to his son."

" I am not surprised," said Neville, " that his father should be so fond of him. He is his heir, his only son, and a man gifted with singular power of attaching those about him. The servants seem to simply adore him."

So talking, the three reached the gate of

Cedar Lodge, and Mrs Winstanley, standing behind her own, on the opposite side of the wide roadway, heard Miss Neville say as they were parting,—

" You will come and see us, then, Mrs Albany, whenever you can, or like ? "

" I shall be so happy, Miss Neville. I think, when I am driving out, the horses will soon learn their way here."

" Upon my word ! " said Mrs Winstanley, " I—I—the horses indeed ! as if the whole thing belonged to her. She steps into that victoria as if she had never been used to anything but a carriage all her life ! Such airs ! "

Which, in fact, Leicester Albany's wife had been more or less. She was " to the manner born," in truth ; but it did not seem that unfortunate Mrs Albany could please Mrs Winstanley in any way, whether she said " we " or " I " only. Alas ! for the Doring lady's censure ! I'm afraid that it was like the account of the Papal excommunication in the "Ingoldsby Legends":—

> "Never was heard such a terrible curse ;
> But what gave rise
> To no little surprise,
> Nobody seemed one penny the worse !"

CHAPTER XIV.

RETURN HOME.

DOUGLAS GLEN-LUNA was back again on his usual couch, in his favourite place by the window, on Monday morning. Not, though, until Dr Neville had been, and given permission for the resumption of his accustomed ways. Wicked Douglas had tried in vain to coax his "fair autocrat." to suffer any remove without orders from headquarters.

"And as to Harford," said Douglas, "I don't believe he would have obeyed any order of mine on the subject if Mrs Albany had even looked a 'No!'"

Gabrielle smiled, and Neville asked when the family returned.

"About midday, I suppose, Dr Neville; as we have not heard."

"And the lift will be ready to use to-morrow."

"So Boyd promised, and you see he has the men hard at work."

"I see. Well, Mr Glen-Luna, I shall expect to meet you and Mrs Albany out with those blood horses again; and in another twelve months, perhaps, we shall reverse the case, and have you driving her on the box-seat of your four-in-hand."

The blood flushed to Douglas's brow; but it died as suddenly, with a look of intense pain and a restless movement.

"Ah, don't! Don't jest!"

"Jest! How could I on such a matter! I was never farther from jesting in my life, Mr Glen-Luna; and I have every hope that, with Mrs Albany's continued assistance, I shall make good my words, under the treat-

ment we shall follow; of which I will speak
more in a few days."

Douglas turned aside, and his breast
heaved.

A year! Only a year, and then—could
it be possible! Dared he look at such a
hope!

"Well, good-bye, Mr Glen-Luna," came
the physician's bright, cheering voice. "I
wish I left all my patients in as good hands
as I do you!"

"I must not forget your good opinion,
then."

He laughed, shook hands with both, and
was gone.

But it was not till afternoon that Sir
Arthur and his wife and daughter came
home; and shortly afterwards a footman
came to inquire if Mr Douglas could see
them.

"Yes, James."

Gabrielle Albany was leaning lightly on
the head of the couch as greetings passed

and anxious questions were asked. It was neither the frank, fine old baronet or his daughter whom her covert searching gaze watched; but that little lady, who kissed her "dear boy" so affectionately, and was so full of gratitude for his escape, to Providence and dear Mrs Albany, who had done *everything* that was right; and what caused the accident, and—

"Indeed, Lady Glen-Luna, it little matters, since," said Gabrielle, dismissing the subject of the accident, "there is a new lift, and very good care must be taken that no second accident occurs."

"And meanwhile, Jessie," said Douglas gravely, "you will have the fullest opportunity of flirting with Dr Chandos Neville."

"Ha! ha! You're as wicked as ever, my boy," laughed Sir Arthur; and Jessie retorted,—

"I shall have better than that, sir, I can tell you, Mr Impudence; for mamma says we're going to town in a few days for the rest of the season, and there'll be plenty of people to flirt with then."

"A highly-to-be-desired end, my dear, I admit, and one in which, I think, few young ladies require lessons. Do they, Adeline?"

"Or men either, you bad boy? But, Arthur, we mustn't tire him. So you fancy, dear boy, by the way, to have Dr Neville to attend you?"

Mrs Albany bent over the sofa head, and laid her finger playfully but imperatively on Douglas's lips.

"Hush! or the doctor will scold me for letting you tire yourself. Please, Lady Glen-Luna, don't make him talk. Indeed, I am afraid I must turn you all out now."

"Oh, you autocrat!" laughed Adeline, "I suspect you will lead my poor Douglas a sad life of it; but of course it is all right. I suppose Dr Neville thinks that it will take some time of medical care to really sound the mischief of—"

"The accident," said Gabrielle quietly.

" Exactly so ; a work of time. It might have been beyond all time."

" Don't talk of it," said Sir Arthur, huskily. " Good-bye, for the present, my own boy."

Douglas clasped his father's hand closely, endured Adeline's kiss and Jessie's caress ; and, when the door closed behind them, said very quietly,—

" Come here, Mrs Albany."

She moved round to his side, never flinching for one moment under his intense searching gaze, as he said,—

" Why did you put your hand on my lips, just now, and answer, or rather take up, Adeline's questioning remarks as you did, fair Jesuit ? "

" My reason was strictly true, Mr Douglas ! and you, like myself, believe in casuistry, I know. I suffered a mistaken impression ; *populus vult decipi decepiatur,*" with a slight shrug of her shoulders and a half smile on her lips.

" *C'est ça,*" said he, his great grey eyes still watching her. " I saw at once that you did not wish the truth about Neville to be known, and so obeyed your lead; for if speech is silver, silence is golden; but I do not see your reason — your motive."

"Will you trust me that it is a good one?" she said steadily. " More than that, will you promise me to still preserve you golden silence, and let them all think that Dr Neville's attendance is only in consequence of this accident, and let me write to him to do the same? I am asking a great deal, I know; but one strong reason I can give you and him is a very self-evident one. It would fret you frightfully and retard your recovery to be talked over, questioned, watched—however kindly meant—gossiped over."

" Saints above! It would madden me!" he said passionately; " do what you like, you are always right!"

Her hand trembled as it touched his gratefully for a second, and the touch suddenly thrilled every fibre of that man's whole being, as she sat down to his escritoire and began to write her letter.

Ah me; for the cruel hand and ruthless schemer that cared not if it made wreck of two human hearts to gain its end ! Would it win in the losing — or — lose in the winning ?

That letter was sent to Cedar Lodge by Marston that evening. Chandos read it, and handed it to his sister, saying quietly,—

" Read it, and burn it, Rose ; she wishes you to see it."

She could be trusted, he knew well.

" She is perfectly right," said Sister Rose, as she burned the letter in a taper, " and her reason shows her to be a true metaphysician. She is a clever woman. Don't you think so, Chandos ? "

" Yes, Rose ; a very clever woman."

The answer was meditative, even abstracted.   Sister Rose added,—

"There is some thought in the back of your mind, Chandos."

He looked up with a half laugh.

"I don't know that there was, dear; certainly nothing definite enough to put into words without sounding too strong for the vague impression I would express. The story of that singular woman's life is no ordinary one, I am sure, and will be no ordinary one."

"I think," said Rose Neville strongly, "that it is a cruel thing to go away and leave her alone to have her very name talked away in this scandalising town. She will leave, and what will you do for your patient?"

"My dear," said Neville serenely, "I agree with you in your first count, but for the other I have no fear at all of Mrs Albany leaving young Glen-Luna's service for anything but his own dismissal. She is a thorough woman of the world—a thorough cosmopolitan—and I am very much mistaken if she has not known troubles to which anything this stupid little place could do or say would be play-work. When one has beaten through a frightful tempest, the storm in a duck pond is worthy only of haughty indifference."

"If," said gentle Rose, "a woman can ever look with indifference on a breath on her name, unless she is hardened."

"No," said Chandos, "seared a little, perhaps, certainly not hardened ; and, after all, Rose, a thoroughly brave, loyal-hearted woman stands at such an immovable height in her own purity."

"Yes," answered Sister Rose, "but what if she falls to her own conscience, what, if while her actions are unblemished, her heart —her poor human heart—swerves from its loyalty."

"Well," said the doctor, getting up and walking slowly to and fro, " it might be a nice question of ethics, how far it would touch a woman's conscience, even to herself, if she were placed in a position of great temptation, and her heart swerved, not from or with her own will—but against all that will's struggles—despite all her efforts to keep it in its strict line of duty. I think that as long as she fights the battle, as long as she suffers in the heart's straying, she has not, cannot, fall to her own conscience—or her purity of soul be sullied. Of course, I am supposing a position in which the temptation must be endured — not fled from."

"The maintenance of her high standard," said Rose, "would, I fear, have but a shaky foundation if, in her heart and her conscience, her purity came on opposite sides of the shield ; how long would the battle be a battle, the suffering remain suffering, in a strong impassioned nature ? You do not mean that if a wife with every excuse loves another man— "

" I mean this, Rose," said the doctor, stopping before her chair, " that if she does not yield to it, and if the love is in itself pure, she is untouched—her pure loyalty is intact. A thought or feeling may be wrong, sinful, but we do not become sinners to it till we meet it, take it in, make it our own."

" You are quite right, Chandos," said Rose, after a pause, " yes, you are quite right. But God help the woman or man who has such a battle to fight ; it might not be won. It is a cruel, cruel thing, Chandos."

She came back with that to where she had started, and shook her head sadly to herself.

They had each, all through, had two living beings before them, and each knew it, though neither had put it into words. It is better not sometimes.

CHAPTER XV.

DR NEVILLE LAYS DOWN THE LAW.

BUT Chandos Neville did not meet the tenants of the west wing out driving with the blood horses. Wishing to have a long talk, he waited till the afternoon of the next day, when, having seen all his other patients, he had the time all his own, and started off to the Hall on foot. At the Doring gates of the park, however, the lodge-keeper stopped him with a bright "Good day, sir. Was you going up to the Hall to see Mr Douglas?"

"Yes, Mrs Crane. Is he out driving?"

"No, sir; but he ain't in the house this fine day, for Mr Harford he's just ridden through, and he told me that the master and Mrs Albany are just down by the river, along near the boathouses."

" Thanks ! Which is the shortest way to that part, then ? "

The woman pointed to a lovely bit of wooding.

" Just through that wood, sir ; and, as soon as you catches sight of the river, turn your back to the Hall and lawns, and keep straight down to the water; then skirt it till you see the master, sir."

Dr Neville thanked her again, and followed her directions, which soon brought him out by the river ; and he had not gone far when he caught the gleam of something crimson between the rich green of the foliage, and the musical murmur of voices came to his ear. Neville made a slight detour, and paused on a rising ground crowned with stately trees, from which he could see the group in the lovely dell below, where the river rippled almost at their feet.

Douglas Glen-Luna was leaning back in his wheeled chair, his attitude the very perfection of easy grace, the sunlight falling full on his handsome face as it turned intent and rapt to his beautiful attendant, who, seated at his feet on the chair, was reading aloud, and it was her crimson scarf which he had seen.

As Chandos paused, the reader seemed to have come to the end of what she was reading, and she looked up in Douglas's face with a question that came distinctly on the clear summer air.

" What would you like next ? "

" Nothing, Mrs Albany. I feel a perfectly selfish wretch already ; but—you read so exquisitely."

She laughed a little, amused, it seemed, at the first words.

" *You* selfish ! I don't think any one can lay that to your charge."

"Then I fear I must be a hypocrite to have given you such an opinion of me.

Don't you think most of my sex are selfish
—more so than women? Candour, now
please, fair Jesuit, if you can."

"I think most men are more selfish than
women ; but," said Gabrielle, smiling, and
looking straight in his face, "if you will
have absolute candour, I do not think you
know what the word selfishness means!"

"Basta!" said he, laughing and colouring. "You cannot tell. You have only
known me a week."

"A feather will show which way the wind
blows, Mr Douglas," Gabrielle answered.
"What shall I read?"

"Nothing yet, chère madame. I cannot
tire you. Ah! who is that?"

Both turned as the doctor's step advanced ;
and the next moment Gabrielle rose quickly,
and Douglas exclaimed joyously,—

"Why, it is our Æsculapius himself!
Soyez toujours le bien venu Neville! Did
you come this way by chance?"

"No, I came after you," answered the

physician in his bright way; "the lodge-keeper directed me, and I thought there could hardly be a better opportunity for a quiet talk. I have some theories which I want to put into practice co-existently with the more purely medical treatment. It is of the first I wish to speak. I don't mean," said the doctor, leaning comfortably back against a tree, and folding his arms, "that I have any new or startling theory to offer, but only old theories—old facts, indeed—which I perhaps push to an extreme, though I do not think either of you will disagree with me."

"Go on, please, Neville."

"Well," said the physician, "I don't think, with all our advancement, that we have yet half fathomed the depth and closeness of the connection between mind and body, the intimate and absolute influence which the mental and physical have over each other, both in health and out of health, especially in the latter case, and the greater the power of both, the deeper, the more intense, the influence of each over the other. I think that in medical science there is scarcely any limit to be placed to the influence and reaction of psychology over physiology."

"I thoroughly endorse every word you have spoken!" said Glen-Luna. "I suppose you have always followed that principle of action in your own career?"

"Ay, and the finer strung the nature I have to deal with the more necessary the treatment," said the doctor, so significantly that Douglas laughed.

"Meaning me, of course. Do you think I shall prove rebellious."

"No; but I am afraid that circumstances would do so if I had not an ally ever at your side in Mrs Albany. We mean to make a complete revolution in your life."

"I think that is done already," said Douglas softly; "but I beg your pardon; go on."

"It is only just begun a week ago," returned the physician decidedly; "and pardon me if it is necessary for me to ask a few questions, which I fear must pain you."

A quick-drawn breath, a quick, transient flush, and a restless movement of one hand as he answered,—

"Say what you like, Neville."

"Thank you.   From the time of the accident, then, you have been left alone, to suffer and brood, and go half-mad with restlessness and agony of mind and body; where you should have had constant and affectionate companionship you have been cruelly neglected.   The mere physical confinement was enough to weaken and injure the body and chances of recovery (which must depend so much on the strength), without the added weight of such mental wear and tear.   A wild, free spirit, a mind used to revelling in the broad expanse of the wide world's garden, a splendid physique,

all suddenly crushed down into the narrow
limits of a suite of rooms, feeling your life
wrecked and God-forgotten, shrinking more
and more morbidly from every one. Mrs
Albany saw—read—all this in a few hours,
and first, in fact, broke through the cordon
when she drove you out last Friday. You
are not probably yourself aware how im-
measurably lowered is your whole physique
from the constant fret of mind acting on it,
and it will take months, perhaps, of a totally
opposite treatment to bring back something
like its native strength,—a treatment which
mainly aims at restoring the physical tone
through restoring the mental tone. Without that—of which Mrs Albany is so in-
tegral a part—I should not have dared to
offer the hope I have. You are like a very
fine instrument thoroughly out of tune. It
cannot be strung up all at once. My plan
is social as well as medical."

He paused. Mrs Albany did not move.
Douglas Glen-Luna, without dropping the

hand he had put over his eyes, said in a very low voice,—

"I know too well how bitterly right you are. What is your plan?"

"Simply, Glen-Luna, to continue and expand what your young friend here has begun. We must 'rub' out, and date from Mons. You have been kept lying down and in one or two positions too much. You shall move positions and recline as much as you are able to bear it. You must go out—be out constantly—and you must no longer shun people, the world, and shrink from it. And as you cannot yet go to society, we must bring society to you. We must get them to bring down guests this autumn."

"No! no! not that, Neville!" Douglas broke out passionately. "I cannot mix with others, meet others I have known, so, so differently."

Soft fingers clasped his—a soft voice, full of the very pathos of intense sympathy, said quietly,—

"It will only be so hard at first, and then you will feel all in your own element again."

He made no answer, or even movement, for some moments; then lifted himself a little, and, closing one hand round hers, held the other out to Chandos.

"Forgive me, Neville. I will never gainsay one wish of yours or hers; it only proves how right you are, and what a coward I have become."

"No, no, not a coward," Chandos interrupted, "you must not be too severe on yourself, or Mrs Albany will scold you."

"I am not afraid of her, tyrant though she is," said Douglas. "Neville, will you turn back to the Hall with us, and let me introduce you to my people?"

"With great pleasure."

They were, in fact, only a short distance from the old Hall, which had been built near the river. Gabrielle rose, came quietly behind the light, dainty chair, and laid her hands on the handle, saying, as Chandos would have taken it from her,—

"Thanks, Dr Neville, but please let me push it as usual; see how light it is and easy.   Indeed, I like it; it is no effort."

That this was true was self-evident the moment she pushed the chair; even up the gentle slope it gave her unmistakably no great exertion, and the physician's practised eye took note that, slight built though she was, every muscle, every fibre was full of a steel-like subtle strength that was almost masculine; and, under strong excitement or passion, might indeed put forth a power which might even rival a man's strength. The thought crossed him then—and before many months had passed, he had cause to remember that thought.

CHAPTER XVI.

READ THE RIDDLE NEAR HOME.

THE dainty chair, with its elastic webwork of fine springs and noiseless - tyred wheels, came along the marble terrace and stopped before the windows of the room where Sir Arthur, after a long ride, sat half-dozing, while Jessie read a novel, and Lady Glen-Luna, seated half behind the window curtains, was drawing the gorgeous silks through her embroidery, her own face and manner as silky as the threads she wove. But she had seen them coming, and almost before Douglas's flute-like tones had called "Adeline," her pretty little ladyship had tripped out, all smiles and welcome, with white, frank hand outstretched to the physician.

"I won't pretend to need the farce of an introduction, Dr Neville," said smiling lip and clear metallic voice. "I should guess who you were, even if I had not heard so much of you. I guessed the moment I saw you all three that it could only be Dr Neville with my dear Douglas."

Chandos bent low over the white, cold hand as he answered that he was pleased to meet her; but Gabrielle, from her vantage place behind the chair, noticed that the hazel eyes scanned her as keenly as covertly the moment she appeared, a fact which Douglas also saw, as Adeline turned to call her daughter and husband.

Jessie caught a very quiet, wicked look from Douglas as her mother performed the introduction, and then hearty, handsome Sir Arthur came out to the group.

"I am so very glad to have met you, Dr

Neville," he said cordially, and the contrast between his and his wife's manner struck three of those present as absolutely ludicrous; "and I am sure I could not wish my son in better hands than yours. I wish you could persuade him not to be such a recluse; more society, I am certain, would—"

"Oh, Sir Arthur!" exclaimed Mrs Albany, laughingly, "please don't make him medical again. Indeed, Dr Neville," lightly striking his arm with that inimitable, charming imperativeness which a handsome, thoroughly accomplished woman of the world knows so well how to use, "you shall not answer now."

"I must e'en obey a lady's command," said Chandos, bowing, "and only beg Lady Glen-Luna to be my defender. I hear you are going to desert the Park for five or six weeks."

"Yes, we go to town to-morrow, I think; and when we return I hope we shall have the pleasure of seeing both yourself and your sister. You see," said my lady, with her frank, merry laugh, "that I have heard of her, too, in the village; I am such a little chatterbox, you know."

"Mamma is frank about her delinquencies," said Jessie; "is she not?"

"Well, Miss Glen-Luna, but chatterboxes enliven the world, and so we must not call it a delinquency. But I fear I must take leave now," as the clock on the tower chimed out four. "You ladies have beguiled me."

"Must you run away so soon," said Sir Arthur and Adeline together; "cannot you stop longer?"

"You are very kind; I cannot, indeed," he answered, and took leave with a very odd impression on his mind; firstly, that in the diversion Gabrielle had made to his reply to Sir Arthur, there had been a far different motive to that which lay so fairly on the surface; and secondly, that she was relieved when he walked away.

But he had not gone more than just beyond the reach of even Douglas's keen ear shot when Gabrielle suddenly exclaimed,—

"*Ma foi!* how provoking! I have forgotten to send my message to his sister after all! Please excuse me a few minutes, Mr Glen-Luna."

Douglas bowed, and leaned back, watching the slight, graceful figure rapidly moving; while the others re-entered the room, declaring it was "too hot in the sun."

"Hot!" said Douglas, shrugging his shoulders; "it never is in England!"

"I think, my dear, that you and Mrs Albany are salamanders," laughed his stepmother through the windows.

Meanwhile Chandos Neville had seen Gabrielle, as she neared him, and instantly turned to meet her, asking quickly,—

"Is anything the matter, Mrs Albany?"

"Not as you mean, Dr Neville; but—can you spare me a few moments?"

"As many as you please!" he answered gravely.

She stood for a minute looking down, her fingers twisting and untwisting her watch guard. She was on dangerous ground, and, knowing it, meant him to show his colours first. Hers was the most subtle nature; his the more candid.

"Dr Neville, I owe you an apology for my interruption a few minutes back. I am afraid that it puzzled and vexed you; that you perhaps misunderstood me."

She lifted those searching eyes of hers straight to his as she spoke.

"Certainly not vexed, dear Mrs Albany," said Chandos earnestly; "not misunderstood, I fancy, for I felt that you had some good reason for your apparently laughing words; puzzled, because I could not quite see your motive."

"No! You were going to thoroughly

endorse Sir Arthur's words; add that
society, a house full of guests, was the very
thing his son should have, *en fin*, show your
tactics."

" Why not? Sir Arthur, I am certain,
and so are you, would do anything for his
son's welfare."

" Certainly he would; but," she looked
down again, with an odd, comical, significant smile about her delicate, firm lips,
" don't you remember the story told of
the Duke of Marlborough at the council of
war ? "

" You mean the one where he had secret
information that a spy was present, and so
gave out a totally opposite plan to his real
scheme, despite all remonstrances."

" *Precisément,* monsieur. Read the
riddle near home—*et voila tout !* I leave
that to your quick wits; to mine the task
of Marlborough. I only ask you to remember how wisely the ancients placed
Truth at the bottom of a well; and leave

the rest to me. I think I am more than a match for the enemy; and I think I read your impression."

"I knew that," said Chandos strongly, "metal upon metal — false heraldry. I cannot think either that Douglas Glen-Luna is deceived."

"Not for one moment," said Gabrielle emphatically, "but he makes no sign. Now we understand each other, Dr Neville."

"Perfectly, and we have one end in view."

"One end. Now adieu, and warn your sister. Will you bring her to see us soon, if she will come?"

"Nothing will give her greater pleasure, Mrs Albany."

He raised his hat, bowed low, and went on, while she returned to Douglas Glen-Luna. He gave her such a keen searching look that she could scarcely bear it, and the colour tinged the soft dark cheeks.

"I beg your pardon," he said quietly;

" shall we go back under the trees, now please, if you are not tired ? "

" I am not at all tired, Mr Douglas. I have taken a liberty with your name ; do you know ? "

" I am only happy if my name can be of any use to you, sweet nurse. What have you done with it ? "

" I have asked Miss Neville to come and see us."

He winced at that, and did not answer. She bent down a little as she pushed the chair.

" Forgive me ! It grieves me to probe a wound and cause suffering, but there must be a beginning, you know."

" I know you are always right, and I wrong," said Glen-Luna, dropping his curly head back on the cushions to look up in her face. " I am afraid you will find me a handful to manage, after all, Mrs Albany."

But Gabrielle only shook her head and laughed.

"An open foe is nothing. It is the secret enemy that one must needs dread."

Did he know that as well as she did? Did she not know that he did, or why had he never once asked a question about any one thing that had passed since she came there? Silence was golden to both unless the serpent's fang came too close, and then—what then?

CHAPTER XVII.

"NOUS AVONS CHANGE TOUT CELA."

A STILL, heavy, brooding evening, sultry and oppressive, the atmosphere charged with that subtle electricity, which is cantly and most incorrectly called "thundery," and few of those who made units of the thousands ever passing to and fro the busy streets of mighty London, but could have predicted a heavy storm before many hours had passed.

Every breath of air—even

"Summer evening's latest sigh,
That shuts the rose."

had died away at sunset, and across the
deep blue vault above, with its myriads
of starry worlds, there lay like a slum-
bering giant overhead, with sweeping robe,
and arms outstretched over the great
city, a mass of lurid clouds, dark and
ominous, flecked a little here and there
with fleecy white that had caught the
last glow of the sunlight, as the wings of
the stormy petrel at sea catch its glint—
wondrous and most awesome beauty in
those far-off heavens—and yet how many
of those restless, surging thousands below,
bent on business or pleasure, paused once
and glanced up to admire? Certainly not
that tall, powerfully-built man—whom we
should know—for he only looked up as
he leaped out of a hansom in Great Portland Street, to mutter a curse on the
close heat.

He was in evening dress, beneath the
light summer wrap coat which he wore,
so it seemed an odd place to alight—still

more odd that he turned at once down
the first eastward outlet, and in a short
while made his way into the quiet bye
street into which, only shortly before, he
had followed Gabrielle Albany. At that
same house, kept by worthy little Mrs
May, Leicester Albany once more stopped,
with a somewhat blank look as he saw a
neat card in the parlour window, with
" Furnished apartments " on it.

" The devil ! " he muttered angrily,
" where's the bird flown ? If it were only
out off England—only off with some lover,
I'd be down on her, and try at least to
get rid of her. I'll find out, though, where
she is."

He went up the steps and knocked.
Mrs May herself answered it, for she had
seen a well-dressed gentleman pause outside, and had an eye to business. His
very first words, however, urbanely enough
spoken, disabused her of any such idea, and
caused a revulsion in her quick little head.

"You lately had a lady lodging here named Albany, I think?"

Mrs May was on her guard at once, and pursed her lips, eyeing the stranger aslant with no friendly expression.

"Mrs Albany left me over a fortnight ago, sir," she said curtly, but civilly. "I was sorry to lose her too."

"Indeed! had she been with you long, then?"

"She kept on my rooms for two years, though she was much abroad herself."

"Was she? And she has left London, you say?"

"I didn't say nothing of the sort, sir," returned Mrs May sharply. "I said she'd left me, and that's all I knows."

"You don't know where she has gone?"

"No, I don't."

He did not believe her—he was furious at the flat denial, and said, with an evil sneer, "I suppose, then, my good woman, that you do not know either that Mrs

Albany left her husband in California about two years ago—fled, I mean, with a lover, and came here and humbugged the law into giving her a separation with a cooked-up case."

Mrs May blazed out at once all in one breath of wrath.

" I wish she could 'a cooked *you* up, I do, for daring to tell such lies ! Upon my soul and body, I don't believe your nothink better than her scamp of a husband his own self, and if hever you come here again, I'll give you in. charge for deferation of character, I will, you nasty, mean wretch, you."

Bang went the door right in his face, and he could hear the little woman's step stumping angrily away within. His own face was livid as he turned away into the street, and he laid this up as another count against his wronged wife.

But smooth and urbane, and handsome once more was Mr Leicester Albany, when

not long afterwards he lounged into the
stylish stalls of the Prince of Wales's,
glanced round, and relapsed into the velvet
seat, with a nod to one or two young men
who were two or three rows behind.

"Who the deuce is that dashing-looking
card, Rosslyn?" asked the young man who
had not been noticed. "I saw him on the
Row last week, and he came out of Aylmer's
salon de jeu last night just as I was
leaving—a new face surely this last fortnight!"

Percy Rosslyn was one of those sort of
society flies who are always more or less
posted up as to the who's-who of the leaves
and twigs eddying about on the restless
waters of London society.

"Yes, a new face," he said; "an awfully
jolly fellow too, and plenty of money—not
a bad catch for some girl who wants a good
settlement; some one introduced Clifford
Brandon at the Polyglot, and he and I
rather struck up an acquaintance."

" How is it that he's such a stranger to London ? " said the younger, in his first season. " He's nearer forty than thirty if he's a day."

" Oh, it's only lately that he's come into a fortune," returned Rosslyn ; " he's been abroad, and in California a good deal, but he says he's tired of roughing it, and means to enjoy his aunt's money in the civilised world."

" Time he did," returned young Saltoun, who did not at present appear quite as *entiché* by Mr Clifford Brandon as the helter-skelter son of Colonel Rosslyn, for such Percy was. " You must introduce me though, Ross."

" All right. Ah, Jove ! there are some people I know," bowing low towards a box to the right. " Didn't know *they* were in town,—Lady and Miss Glen-Luna."

" Deuced pretty, both of them," commented Saltoun, " especially the daughter. I say, Brandon's twigging them too, and saw you bow. Whew! how frightfully hot it is!"

An opinion evidently shared by every one in the theatre, to judge by the faces, and the indefinite—ah—of breath when the gas was lowered as the curtain rose again, and a puff of air, somewhat sirocco-like certainly, came from the stage. A few moments later, while inimitable Mrs Bancroft chained the attention of the house, there came a deep growl of thunder above, as if the cloudy monster afar had roused himself at last; then a flash that gleamed like daylight through the windows behind the gallery, and then a roar, a crash that shook the very roof and walls of the building, and seemed as if the whole mighty canopy of heaven were rent in twain. A woman in the gallery uttered a half shriek, aud cried out that the theatre was struck and would take fire! There had been an upward look instantly—an upheaving of fear through the audience—there would possibly have been a panic, but Leicester Albany, tall and imposing, stood up for a moment, glanced towards the gallery, and, as if speaking to some one near him, said quietly, but aloud and distinctly,—

" They don't seem to know that there is a very lofty lightning conductor on the roof."

The crowd settled, every ear heard, every eye turned on the speaker as he resumed his seat. Rosslyn said audibly, " Well done, Brandon," and Jessie Glen-Luna whispered enthusiastically to her mother, " What a dear fellow, mamma ! Isn't he handsome ? Do make Percy Rosslyn introduce him. I saw him nod to him."

" We'll see, my dear ; if he knows the Rosslyns at all, we are certain to meet him, for the Colonel and his wife are in town too. Ah ! another clap of thunder ! How dreadful ! And *so* hot !" fanning herself languidly, " I shall be glad when the curtain falls."

" I wish we had not come at all," said

Jessie. " I'm dreadfully afraid of being out in a thunder storm."

The storm, too, was near, for the roll of thunder was almost ceaseless; and before the end of the last act Lady Glen-Luna suggested departing. Jessie rose and followed her out. Some others were leaving also, but, on receiving the name at the entrance, the policeman soon brought up the carriage. The thunder had rolled for some minutes, though the heavens were now a mass of lurid electric clouds as Albany, coming towards the entrance with his wrap-coat over his arm, saw—saw those two ladies again, too, and noticed that the elder had diamonds in her ears.

" Lady Glen-Luna's carriage ! "

In that moment, as Jessie stepped forward to reach it, there was a sudden crash of thunder overhead—a gleam, a flash of forked lightning, so fearfully dazzling, so close, that every one started back with hands to their eyes—Jessie, with a wild shriek of frantic terror; her skirt was just alight, and with that shriek she was rushing madly forward, half blinded, courting the very death or injuries she fled, when, with one leap, Albany seized her in his powerful grasp, wrapped his overcoat close around her limbs, crushed the great door mat over that, and so completely smothered the flame beyond the portion of dress and underskirt. It was all the work of a minute, and poor little Jessie, really unhurt, but more than half fainting with terror — hearing the shrieks of the women and her mother's voice, as in a dream, was lifted in those strong arms and borne to the carriage — placed at her mother's side.

"You will permit me to escort you safe home, madam?" said Albany, seeing that the mother was as white and almost as shaken as the daughter, and, hardly waiting for her trembling,—

"Thank you—I cannot trouble you," stepped in, and the carriage dashed off, leaving the crowd to stare and the storm to rage; for now the heavens were opened and the rain came down in a deluge.

Leicester drew up both windows, and bent forward as Jessie began to revive, under her mother's strong salts.

"I do not think the flame reached her," he said gently. "I cannot but be thankful for the chance that brought me out before the end. I went to catch my friend, Percy Rosslyn."

"You have saved my child's life!" said Adeline, for once with real warmth, real earnest sincerity and feeling—for this girl was the one thing she did care for—"and I do not know how to thank you enough!"

"Indeed, madam, you make too much of the slight service it has been my good fortune to render your daughter."

"Ah, you may make light of it! but her mother and father, nor she herself, cannot be so ungrateful. Who are we to thank?" and Jessie's blue eyes, as she lay against her mother, looked up in his with a mute entreaty. How bewitching she looked!

"My name is Clifford Brandon. Very much at your service, Lady Glen-Luna."

"Thank you! I saw you come in and bow to young Rosslyn." Adeline added, "His father's place is only ten miles from our own, at Doring."

Albany bowed, and secretly thanked his lucky stars. If only this pretty little thing were an heiress!

The carriage presently stopped at a handsome house in Park Lane, and Mr Leicester Albany—for we will still give him his own name—assisted the fair Jessie out.

"You will do us the pleasure of calling to-morrow, I hope, Mr Brandon," said Adeline, cordially shaking hands; "and the carriage shall take you on home now. Nay, I insist on it!"

"You must, indeed!" added Jessie languidly, but with a sweet smile; and, bowing low, Gabrielle's husband accepted and re-entered the carriage, giving the direction to his chambers in Grafton Street, where a handsome douceur to my lady's coachman, made that worthy decide "him to be every inch a gentleman."

Certainly, Mr Leicester Albany had not done a bad stroke of business for himself that night.

And so he himself thought.

CHAPTER XVIII.

THE NEXT MORNING.

MR LEICESTER ALBANY was certainly not one of those modest gentlemen who are content to blossom and bloom in unobtrusive, unrecognised virtue. He was the last man likely to lose a chance windfall or miss an opportunity for want of that inimitable quality, which perhaps no lexicon so exactly describes as the very terse, if not equally elegant slang word "cheek." He was perfectly aware of the value of that quality, used as he so well knew how to use it, in addition to his personal advantages. He saw as clear as daylight that he had made a very decided impression on this Lady Glen-Luna and the fair girl he had unquestionably rescued from at least a terrible injury, if not death. The introduction was out of the beaten track, romantic; and, if he had not much of the substance left, he could assume the mask of sentiment enough to deceive the most of the world. His scornful wife had only spoken truth in the stern irony of her words—

" In birth, appearance, manners, you are a gentleman—in nothing else."

But it was the first he kept before the world; the latter he hid.

" It only remains to ascertain her prospects," quoth Gabrielle's admirable husband dryly, " to mark her as my quarry. Pretty little thing, by Jove! and I am certain, easy to twist round my finger, which ' l'adorata Gabriella' never would be, curse her, even as a slip of sixteen. So now for Percy Rosslyn."

He completed an adjustment of dress before the mirror with an extreme, almost foppish attention, to an effective appearance, and took his departure in a most halcyon state of self-satisfaction.

"By Jove, you are in luck, you are, Cliff Brandon!" was young Rosslyn's first salute. "I've just heard all about that affair last night. Haven't you just cut everybody out with that little heiress!"

"Heiress, is she?" said Albany, carelessly, as he dropped into a chair. "Is she an only child, then?"

"Well, it comes to that, I suppose, practically, my dear fellow—try one of those cigars; for, though there is a son by a first marriage, he can't live long. Got awfully smashed, you know, in some railway accident ages ago. He's dying by inches, I believe; so somebody said, t'other day, at the Bijou."

"Poor devil!" said Albany, lighting a

cigar. "I nearly got smashed once—ugh! So this girl is—"

"Heiress of all the broad Glen-Luna lands, after her brother!" said Rosslyn; "and, if she wasn't, I don't believe she'd have such a contemptible dower."

"Still dowers don't generally run to much," returned his companion. "Not that I care myself. Dame Fortune has been kind to me on the whole, so that I can please myself. I am going to call there, as Lady Glen-Luna asked me; and so you may as well come too."

"All right, my boy; I'm agreeable. The two ladies are charming, and Sir Arthur a jolly old fellow."

"What sort of being is this dying son?" asked Albany, as they descended to the street, and turned towards Park Lane.

"What—Douglas Glen-Luna? He was the most splendid fellow you ever saw! The most fascinating man in every way, and everybody's favourite. It's an awful shame! No one has seen him since the accident, of course."

"Where is he, then?"

"Oh, at Luna Park."

"Then, Lady Glen - Luna is his stepmother?"

"Rather, my boy. I don't think she is much over forty, and he is thirty. How do you like her?"

"Charming, I should think. Her daughter is very like her."

"Yes. Jessie isn't a bit of a Glen-Luna; which is a pity, pretty as she is, for if she was, she'd be bound to be a regular beauty. So was the first wife, by her portrait; but, by Venus, Brandon, talk of beauty! I once saw a woman whom I defy any one to rival. I should know her again; quite young; two or three-and-twenty, perhaps. She was with an old blind gentleman, in a box at the opera at Vienna. He was English; she was not, I think."

"It's clear, cher Ross, that you lost your

heart to this *inconnue*," laughed Albany, with the slightest suspicion of a sneer. " What was she like ? "

" My dear fellow, language fails me—tall, slight as a girl, graceful as a houri, rather dark, very pale, features like a statue gifted with vivid life."

" Isn't that tortology ?   But go on."

" And her glorious dark eyes—"

" Which it is evident she used with great effect," again put in Albany.

" She never looked at me, mon cher; though I certainly saw more of her than the stage."

" And how did this beauty dress—wear her hair, my Romeo ? "

" Dress ?—exquisitely, in black velvet and silver ornaments, and her hair was just in rich masses of ripple and curls all over her head, fringing her forehead, falling on to her neck. *Foi!* I tell you she was superb!   You wouldn't look at fifty Jessies after her, I'm sure."

" Perhaps not," said the other dryly. He had recognised his own beautiful wife fast enough, even with such a bald rhapsodical description. " Who was your diva, eh ? "

" Don't know, except that she was somebody's wife, for she wore a wedding-ring. I saw it as she drew off her left glove."

" Somebody should be a very happy man," said Albany, with another sneer, " except for the fact of being her husband."

Rosslyn laughed ; but by this time they had reached the house in Park Lane, and, in reply to their inquiry whether the ladies were at home, were shown up into the drawing-room, where they found not only the two ladies, but Sir Arthur, whose hearty reception of the *soi-disant* Brandon, and heartfelt thanks to him, really meant far more gratitude than the effusive welcome of Adeline, or the slight blush and smile of Jessie, the most arrant flirt, by the way, like her mother before her.

" And you must both come to dinner with us," said Sir Arthur presently, when the accident and fearful thunderstorm had been discussed, " for my wife has asked a few friends, quite a little dinner party this time, to whom we should like to introduce you, Mr Brandon. Do you know Lady Constance Lee and her daughter ? "

" I have not that honour, Sir Arthur," answered Albany, with a glance at Jessie ; " I have not been long in town, you see."

" Indeed ; nor have we. I hate town myself," said the baronet, laughing, " except for a very short time ; but my wife and daughter like to see the gay world, of course, though they're not dull at Luna Park at all."

" Sir Arthur is such a sportsman, Mr Brandon," said Adeline, merrily, " that he hardly feels happy unless he has a gun or something of the sort in his hand. Do you shoot ? "

" Oh yes, Lady Glen-Luna ; I am very fond of sport."

Which quite won Sir Arthur, and the visitors took leave till dinner time.

But the sport Mr Leicester Albany liked best was to be found in certain brilliantly lighted *salons* with cards instead of game. That beautiful woman down at Luna Park could have told that too well.

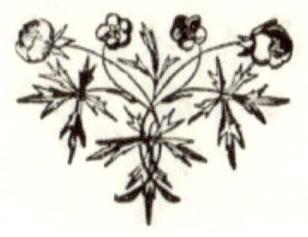

CHAPTER XIX.

SISTER ROSE GOES TO LUNA PARK.

"I WONDER what made Neville bury himself in Doring, even for a few months?"

With that remark, Douglas Glen-Luna broke a long silence, one sunny afternoon. He was lying in his most usual place on the couch, for they had been out all the morning, and he was rather tired; so his "sweet autocrat," as he called her, had banned anything but rest this afternoon.

She had been standing for a long time leaning against the lintel of the window, her hands loosely locked before her, her

eyes fixed dreamily on the fair panorama
of hill and wold and river spread before
their vision, and her thoughts perhaps on
her own sorrowful, stormy past, or perhaps
—heaven help the poor, passionate, human
heart!—on a present very much nearer to
her. So deep had been her reverie, so far
from Chandos Neville, that the sound of
Douglas's voice, low and soft though it
was, made her almost start.

"The same thought has crossed me more
than once," she answered him. "They
have evidently some very fair private
means, and had a practice in London.
Indeed, from a remark he made the day
after your family left, I fancy he runs up
for one whole day every week."

"Ah, well," said Douglas contentedly,
"whatever the reason, it is fortunate for
me that he came, and that the lift broke,
too, however that happened."

It was the first time he had voluntarily
made any allusion to the cause of that acci-

dent, and now, as he said it, he looked straight into her face. She met that searching look without the quiver or droop of an eyelid, and answered,—

" It was a very perilous curse of Kehama ; and if it has turned into a blessing, it was never—"

She stopped short, setting her teeth sharply, and added with a shudder that was real enough,—

" Don't talk of it—it was too terrible ! I wish Miss Neville would call." Gabrielle moved now to her little, low easy-chair, near the couch. " Do you know that she reminds me always of Nathaniel the Israelite, in whom was no guile."

" Does she ? Mrs Albany, do you ever —I am sure you do—in your own mind liken or identify people you know with their prototypes in music, those that have anything marked about them at all ? "

" Oh yes, often ! Sometimes to a class of music, sometimes to a particular thing."

Glen-Luna smiled, playing with his moustache. It was evident that he had assigned a musical prototype to his companion.

" Well," he said, " and what, then, is this ' Sister Rose,' as her brother calls her ? "

Gabrielle glanced up under the long lashes.

" I don't know what you would think of her ; but to me, she is the very personification of the divine Felix's exquisite ' Calm and prosperous voyage.' "

" Your very contrast, then," said Douglas impulsively. " For you, Rubinstein's gorgeous, passionate ' Ocean' symphony is your very self. Ah ! pardon me. My thoughts escaped too fast into words, Mrs Albany."

" No, no ! Why should it not ? Who indeed, should so well hold free interchange of thought, if not those who are constant companions, as we necessarily are? Where did you hear that magnificent work?"

"Where? Well, abroad; the very first time of its performance. I wish you had been there, dear Mrs Albany!"

Gabrielle laughed.

"How do you know I was not?"

"Ah, you were, I do believe!" exclaimed Douglas; "were you not?"

"Yes, I was there."

"I wonder," he said, with a restless movement, "if I shall ever really be in a concert room again, and with you. I dare not hope — think — of the future, sometimes."

"I can feel exactly how you feel," said Gabrielle gently; "but that painful dread, that very fear of hope will lessen as you grow stronger, and have more people about you again."

"*En effet*, you think the instrument has gone thoroughly out of tune." But his smile was sad. "I think you will do more to tune it than a score of people."

"Shall I? But here, I think, comes one who will help," said Mrs Albany, as some one opened the anteroom door, and a footman entered, bearing a card on a tiny silver salver which he handed to his mistress, as Douglas's own household had speedily learned to regard Gabrielle Albany.

"Show Miss Neville in, Watson," she said, at once rising to meet the welcome visitor, as the footman ushered her in. "Dear Miss Neville, we have been hoping to see you every day."

"But I suppose," added Douglas, as he shook hands, at once fully endorsing Gabrielle's comparison, "I must not say better late than never."

"Well, I daresay I deserve it, Mr Glen-Luna," said Sister Rose, with her gentle smile, as she took the seat placed for her, "and indeed I meant to have come two or three days ago, only that thunderstorm prevented me. I see by the papers that it burst that night over London with great violence."

"Yes, I daresay I shall hear of it when my people write," answered Glen-Luna. "Why did not your brother come too, Miss Neville? He must not think his early morning visit is ever to count at all, because that is strictly professional."

"I will tell him that, Mr Glen-Luna, and he would have called with me if he had been in Doring, but directly he left you, he went up to town to see how his practice is getting on. You see," said Rose Neville, softly smoothing her white hands over her dress, "that for a long time past Chandos has been overworking between his practice and a very abstruse professional work in which he was engaged, and he is so earnest, you know, so deeply interested in all his work,"—she paused.

"Ay," said Douglas strongly, "his very heart is in his work, if ever man's was!"

The brown eyes thanked him as their owner went on,—

"So it is. Well, at last he got so worn, so overworked in serious earnest, that old Dr M— told him plainly that unless he had rest and change for some months he would have a brain fever. I had been singing the same song for a long time, you know, but,"—said sweet Sister Rose, smiling benignly — "you young people are so proud of your strength and intellect that you never think that it can be overworked; you run till you drop. Ah, you may look so wickedly guilty at Mrs Albany, my dear." How sweetly and naturally the words fell from those patient, peaceful lips. "It is quite true, and I suspect that Mrs Albany is every bit as bad as you or Chandos on such points; you won't listen to reason till it is almost too late."

"Oh, Miss Neville! Miss Neville!" cried Douglas, putting out both his hands, "I shall have to lay lance in rest for both Mrs Albany and myself."

"But you did get the doctor to hear reason, Miss Neville ? " said Gabrielle, with a rather comic glance, and Sister Rose laughed as merrily as a girl.

" Oh yes, my dear ; at last he got a very clever young man for a partner, and we went abroad for a month or six weeks, and then Mr Parker was obliged to go away for a few months for some family reasons, and asked Chandos to come here for him. Of course, the work was very different from his London practice, to which, indeed, he really was not fit to return, at least they all told him he would soon go all back again. A couple of months here will make all right for him. But now, of course, his staying or leaving here will not depend on Mr Parker's return."

" He must not stop here on my account, Miss Neville," said Douglas quickly.

"Hush ! " said Gabrielle, touching his

hand ; and Sister Rose answered, smiling,—

" My dear Mr Glen-Luna, if you wish to
get the most thorough scolding you ever
had in your life, say that to Chandos himself. He has so set his heart upon this
matter, and I never yet knew him put his
hand to the plough and look back ; neither
will a few more months in such lovely
scenery be such a very great hardship."

" Are you fond of the country, Miss
Neville ? " asked Mrs Albany.

The answer was thoroughly character-
istic.

" Very fond of it in summer, my dear ;
and then 1 love gardening, and the sweet
fresh air and peaceful quiet. I am quite
different to you two young people, you see,"
she added, smiling, " and then I have fifty
years ; not that I ever was different though,
or that I mean you will change materially
with years. It is a matter of difference of
nature."

" But you don't, then, prefer the country for headquarters ? " said Douglas.

"Oh dear, no; I like best to live in London, not in the whirl and racket which you people like, but still I am fond of my kind, of the society of those I like. I think, with old John Anderson's wife, that 'God's master-work is man;' though I am not sufficiently gifted with metaphysical power to call myself a student of human nature."

Sweet Rose ! No, she simply followed her instincts and sympathies, and they rarely misled her, if she could not fathom the extreme of evil or passion so foreign to herself, or be capable of fighting out the world's fiercest battle, like Gabrielle Albany.

Miss Neville rose as she said the last words, but Glen-Luna exclaimed,—

" You are not going to run away so soon, dear Miss Neville ? You have no excuse, as your brother is away. Do stop and give us the pleasure of your company for the rest of the day, and Marston shall drive you home."

The pleading grey eyes and entreating hand were irresistible, certainly, even without Gabrielle's eager,—"You must stop, Miss Neville," and Sister Rose yielded by no means unwillingly.

"Then come to my room and take off your things," said her hostess. "Have you dined yet?"

"Will you be shocked if I confess that I dined at two to-day, Mrs Albany?"

"Oh no; we sinned in company, for we, having only our two selves to please, chose to have dinner when we came in from a long drive, so we will have a cosy high tea!"

"It does not matter what dreadful things one does in the country, does it, Miss Neville?" said Douglas, laying back his head, "even cosy high tea at—six? I am ashamed of you, Mrs Albany, really, for encouraging such doings."

" You don't like tea then, I suppose ? " said Rose.

"Oh, *ma foi!* Yes I do, though, Miss Neville, especially from fair hands," returned wicked Douglas, kissing the tips of his fingers to them as they passed out of the room.

Such a cosy pretty tea it was, too, and Sister Rose sat beaming like mellowed sunlight on her two brilliant companions, and feeling as if she had known them for years. Perhaps the feeling was reciprocal. Conversation never flagged, and then, just after the equipage had been removed, the post came in with London letters; one for Douglas, and a little packet, both addressed in Adeline's hand.

He was putting them aside, but Rose Neville arrested his hand.

" Please do not make a stranger of me, Mr Glen-Luna, or I shall fly at once."

" That would be too cruel," was the gallant answer. " *Eh bien,* since you kindly permit me, I will see what the little belle mère has to say of their doings, while madam shows you that album of photographs."

The letter, which began, " My dearest boy," contained a very gushing account of the storm and Jessie's " terrible danger" and " courageous rescue" by a friend of " dear Colonel Rosslyn's son Percy, who had called with him in Park Lane the next day." She enlarged much on the gifts and charms of this Mr Clifford Brandon, whom they all " liked so much." He was quite an acquisition to society, etc. The packet contained some beautiful new photos of herself, Jessie, and Sir Arthur. " And, dear Douglas, I was in such a hurry to catch this post that you might have them quickly, that I wrapped them over the cardboard with a piece of an old newspaper which was in my desk—had some faded photos of Jessie in it—so please excuse such hasty wrapping."

" Your letter seems amusing," said Gabrielle, as he laughed once or twice.

"So it is," said he, deftly tossing the letter into her lap; "it's so like la belle mère.   Please read it to Miss Neville.   I suppose poor Jessie really did have a narrow escape, and the gentleman who saved her has earned our gratitude; but he seems to have quite fascinated Adeline and my dear sentimental little sister.   Do read it; quite a lady's letter, Miss Neville."

"Do you think all ladies write gushingly and in exaggerated language, then?" asked Rose, amused.

"Oh no; I am sure you would not, and I know that a certain Gabrielle Albany does not," returned Glen-Luna, archly; "but you will admit that a great many ladies do.   I really now do not feel at all sure that my sister was so nearly burnt at the theatre door as her mother says, nor will you when you read her letter."

Which while Mrs Albany read aloud, with its many italics, Douglas undid the photos and handed them to the ladies for inspection.

"I must write to little Jessie," he said, "about her escape from that most horrible enemy—fire; besides, I must chaff her about this lady-killer Brandon. She is a rare little flirt, I am afraid, Miss Neville."

"Ah, well, I suppose most young people take their turn," said Sister Rose indulgently, "and we should not wish to put old heads on young shoulders."

He laughed, and shook his head.

"Oh no! Certainly not."

His hand, as he spoke, had been half absently, perhaps a little restlessly, tearing small bits off the top of the very piece of old newspaper wrapping alluded to in the letter; and Sister Rose, pointing to it, said,—

"Pardon me. Is that anything you wish to keep?"

His glance dropped on the print directly. He had torn away the headline and name; but his eye fell upon the words,—

"This was a suit for a judicial separation

on the ground of cruelty. The respondent, when called upon in the usual way, did not appear ; and the cause was, therefore, proceeded with. The petitioner stated—"

Carelessly, more because the quick glance could not fail to take in the summarised report almost all at once, Douglas read it down ; so little dreaming whose most miserable story of wrong upon wrong he was reading. How should he, when he had never heard it ? He threw down the paper with an almost passionate exclamation.

" Look there, Miss Neville ! Man was made a little lower than the angels, we know ; but here is one of those records that might almost induce one to believe, with old Jeremy Taylor, that there are some beings in this world who are verily the offspring of devils and witches ! I should like to have a loaded pistol in my hand, and such a thing as that within range ! "

Gabrielle, who was placing the new photos in an album, looked up with some surprise, asking,—

"What case have you got hold of?" While Rose took it up, glanced through it, and laid the paper down with a look of incredulous horror and an actual shudder.

"It cannot be all true! It is too horrible—a man to actually gamble away his own young wife! Impossible!"

Impossible—was it? Why, then, that sharp, quick start from the beautiful woman sitting there? Why that sudden, burning flush of shame, and as sudden ghastly pallor, that left her very lips bloodless? The truth flashed upon both at once, and Douglas started half up with flashing eyes and passionate words.

"Mrs Albany, forgive me! I never dreamed of this! Saints in Heaven! I would I had the dastard here, to rid the world of such a reptile!"

"Hush! Oh, hush!" said Gabrielle, hoarsely. "I never meant—I—I—" The stern will was struggling fiercely for its wonted mastery; but pitying Sister Rose bent forward with outstretched hands.

"My poor heart! Oh, my poor child!"

And the proud, suffering woman, broken down, knelt suddenly at Rose Neville's feet, and buried her face in her lap; not weeping, but quivering from head to foot with an emotion that would have its own fierce way for many minutes. Then she said, brokenly, very low, as if the bitter shame were hers.

"Forgive me—both! It was only that it brought it all back so, so terribly! I would not have had your noble hearts pained by such a miserable story!" She rose up now; and, putting one hand in Rose's, stretched the other to Douglas, whose clasp closed on it instantly like a vice.

"Thank you!" she said gratefully.

" Will you both, when we are alone, mind simply calling me by my own name, Gabrielle? The other; you understand—and forgive my foolishness!"

Glen-Luna could not, dared not, speak; but only lifted that little hand to his loyal lips. But Miss Neville drew the younger woman to her, and gently kissed her brow.

"So be it, then, dear child; only you must call me Sister Rose."

How like balm on troubled waters came sympathy and love! Oh! if it could only heal that wounded heart, and give back the fair bloom of unseared youth!

But who can undo the past, or read the future aright?

CHAPTER XX.

MOTHER AND DAUGHTER.

"HYACINTH?"

"Well, mamma!"

Mother and daughter unmistakably. There was quite enough indefinite, not actual, likeness to show a near relationship; though the question and witty repartee that is told of the lovely Countess of Chepstow and her daughter would hardly have found point here.

"What would you give for your mother's beauty, my love?" asked the countess.

"Exactly as much as your ladyship would give for my youth," returned the daughter.

But here the daughter had the palm in

both, for Hyacinth Lee, at three-and-twenty, was still—

In the full flowering of her dainty May,

and gifted with a beauty which her mother, good-looking as she was, had never had. She was just now lounging in the laziest of attitudes on the sofa in her mother's boudoir, looking the very picture of saucy, idle contentment. She had a pretty shrewd idea of what lay behind the portentous opening.

" Well, mamma ! "

Lady Constance laid down the " society " paper which she had been reading, and folded her hands on her knees.

" My dear, have you seriously reflected that time does not stand still even for you, and this is your fourth season ? "

" Quite true, mamma. What then ? "

" Well, child, it is time you thought of accepting, not refusing, offers."

Hyacinth pursed up her pretty lips.

"Why is it time, dear? Mr Wright hasn't appeared yet!"

"I think he has several times," returned Lady Constance vexedly. "Why did you refuse Lord Clenham in your first season? He was no fortune-hunter, for he had plenty."

"Didn't like his dear little turned-up nose, mother mine," said the heiress jauntily. "He was so plain, they would have called us Beauty and the Beast!"

"Nonsense, Hyacinth! You know well enough that I don't want you to marry any fortune-hunter just because he is titled, though I do very much wish to see you married to some eligible *parti* of your own rank. A coronet is what you would grace, and yet you have refused I don't know how many!"

"I didn't care one bit for any of them, mamma! I'm of

The eclectic school of thought, which flirts with many ;
　　Too worldly wise to wed itself to any !

I'm not in love, mamma."

"I sometimes think you are, Hyacinth," said Lady Constance, looking straight at her refractory daughter.

"I know you do, dear," said that young lady composedly; "and so I daresay do others. Men are so conceited, that they can't conceive a girl refusing their precious hands, unless some happy swain has been before them. I don't mean to get married for either my beauty or money."

"I tell you what I *do* think, Hyacinth," said Lady Constance, provoked out of all caution, "that you might have had Douglas Glen-Luna at your feet more than two years ago if you had chosen."

"Ah, poor Douglas!" The girl's face clouded suddenly. Then she said, in her old manner, "Firstly, I did not choose, you see, mamma dear, and secondly, *he* didn't choose your humble servant. Very bad taste of him, of course, but still he didn't see it."

"Nonsense, my love! He admired you

immensely, and used to pay you more attention—"

"My dear, self-tormenting mamma of mammas, he never did, or said, or looked, or cared for me one bit more than he did for any other pretty girl he liked, and who liked him. It was only the way of such a careless, cavalier sort of fellow; and we got on so well, just I believe, because I didn't flirt seriously or make him feel that I thought he 'had intentions' like Miggs. I know," she said, breaking into a very amused laugh, "that Lady Glen-Luna (and perhaps others too) rather think I am Hyacinth Lee still for the sake of handsome, winning Douglas Glen-Luna, whom she imagines no young woman can help falling in love with, though he never did himself, favourite as he was."

"If she does," exclaimed Lady Constance, veering round with instantly-stirred maternal indignation, "how dare she think that my daughter is going to throw herself at her stepson's head, just because he admired her!"

"Oh, you dear old goosey! and a second ago you scolded me because I had *not* thrown myself at his head!" cried Hyacinth, laughing heartily, "How do you think this new star of fashion—Mr Clifford Brandon—will do? *On dit*, he's awfully rich, and I'm sure he is a most agreeable fellow, especially to flirt with, and really, I suppose it *is* time I began to seriously look out, or I shall be left on the old maid's shelf,"—this with a sly, saucy gleam of fun in the blue eyes. "Wasn't Jessie wild when he took me to have an ice?"

"I think," said Lady Constance seriously, "that you had better leave Mr Brandon to Jessie. He is well introduced, and rich enough, I daresay, for a Crœsus, and I like him very much." ("Which I don't," muttered Miss Hyacinth, "but he'll do to keep one's hand in and get some fun.") "But

still he's not the *parti* I should choose for
my child."

"Perhaps," thought "my child," pursing
her lips again, " she may choose for herself
some day." Then aloud,—

"Oh, dear me! Why in the world can't
the girls be let alone? Why must they
marry, forsooth! I won't—unless I go
and marry a market gardener, like Dick
Swiveller's adored Sophy Wackles, or some
poor struggling professional creature who—"

"Hyacinth," interposed her mother,
solemnly, "if ever you dream of any such
a *mésalliance*, you will never see my face
again."

"Really, how awful!" Miss Hyacinth
pulled a face a yard long. "I wonder
which of us would hold out the longest?
Not you, mamma."

"Don't you try me, daughter mine,"
returned Lady Constance, shaking her head;
" and don't send Mr Clifford Brandon to
ask me for your hand."

"Oh dear, no, mamma! I should accept or refuse him myself, honour bright, dear. I would not think of troubling you unnecessarily. Ta-ta, now. I promised Jessie Glen-Luna I'd ride with her."

And off tripped the refractory young lady to dress, singing saucily enough,—

> "Oh, I should like to marry,
>   If that I could find
>   A fine young handsome fellow
>   Just suited to my mind."

Sunny bird of spring time! Her life had hitherto been as happy as Gabrielle Albany's had been dark and sorrowful.

END OF VOL. I.

COLSTON AND SON, PRINTERS, EDINBURGH.